The Stronger Half

Jeff Coleman

PALLID VISIONS™

Published internationally by Pallid Visions®

PO box 5943

Buena Park, CA 90622, United States

Cover art and design ©2018 Vincent Chong (http://www.vincentchong-art.co.uk).

This book is a work of fiction. Any similarity between the characters and situations within its pages and places or persons, living or dead, is unintentional and coincidental.

For more information about the author, visit his homepage:

https://blog.jeffcolemanwrites.com/

ISBN 978-1-945997-11-2 (E-book)

ISBN 978-1-945997-12-9 (Hardcover)

ISBN 978-1-945997-13-6 (Paperback)

Library of Congress Control Number: 2018953617

First Edition.

Contents

Acknowledgments

This book is dedicated to my wife, my parents, and my patrons. You all have helped me out so much and in so many different ways. What else is there to say but "thank you!"

As is customary with all my books, I'd like to give a shout out to all of my patrons by name. If you became one after August 6, 2018, I'm sorry I wasn't able to list you here. But know that you, too, hold a special place in my heart, and that this book wouldn't have been possible with you.

Quiarrah

Jill Babbs

AmySue Bortz

Janis Chandler

Anthony Colannino

Voni Colannino

Jeannine Cook-Battles

Brandy Dalton

Julia Davis

Christyne Demos

Cara Eckman

Derrick Elkins

Angela Escarcega

Monica A. Franklin

Anna Garcia-Centner

Melissa Iwata

"JonBoy" Maddron

Susan Malloy

Katina McAllister

Barbara G McCann

Allen Morris

Karen Palumar

Jessica Parkko

Robert Peirson

Jason Peverly

Lisa Plante

Suzie Queen

Alixevette Solstice

Laura Anne StJohn

Karen Sutton

Rae Taylor

Chad Walker

Pat Williamson

1.

April 2017

COLD WATER LAPPED and splashed about George's waist, making him shiver. He glanced back at his identical twin, Bill, whose mouth was contorted into what George had learned to recognize as a smile. As if sensing George's hesitation, Bill let out a guttural plea, a primal sound that signaled he was impatient and wanted to be let in.

"Okay, Bill," said George. "But it's cold."

He reached over the concrete edge of the pool, unstrapped his twin from his wheelchair, and lowered him in.

George took him to the gym every Wednesday and Friday. It was expensive—35 dollars a month was a lot of money for a junior high school janitor already struggling with debt—but Bill loved to swim and needed the recreation.

Bill's mouth twisted further, eyes darting from side to side, and George didn't need the widening lopsided smile to know Bill was enjoying the water. He supported his brother, made extra buoyant by the plastic floaties affixed to his arms and legs, and slowly led him around the perimeter like a float in the Macy's Thanksgiving Day parade.

The sound of snickering made him swivel. By the larger pool, a couple of dopey-faced teenagers were staring in George's direction. When they met his eyes, their smiles evaporated, and they whipped their heads back toward the opposite wall.

George imagined his fist and their faces flying back into the water.

Though Bill's head hadn't turned, and though he continued to make satisfied grunts and groans, George knew he'd heard them. The doctors and his mom had explained that his twin brother's awareness of the world had been impaired along with his speech and fine motor control, but George had never believed them. They hadn't spent most nights with Bill when everyone else was asleep.

From time to time, George would glance down at the surface of the water and watch the shimmering distorted reflection of his brother, a broken version of himself. It wasn't fair that Bill had been the one injured. It should have been him.

They remained in the water for almost forty minutes, until Bill began to flail his arms and groan impatiently. Then George glanced at the clock and realized it was almost nine—nearly Bill's bedtime. He pulled him out, dried him off, and wheeled him into the changing room, where he dressed him in a new diaper, a pair of shorts, and a black T-shirt.

They were heading out the door, George once more brooding over where he was going to get the money to keep up the gym membership, when he spotted a man in a black fedora and suit, leaning up against the wall like a model out of a 1950s cigarette ad.

George sighed. He'd seen the Man before.

He'd started seeing him shortly after Bill's accident. He and his brother would be at the mall and he would catch the Man sitting on a bench. Then they would be at the grocery store and he would spot the Man standing by the magazines. Sometimes, he'd even spot the Man in their parents' yard, ambling about as if he were searching for something he'd misplaced. Once, when he and Bill were at the park, George had sat on a bench next to him and tried to start a conversation. But he'd just looked on, as if George and Bill didn't exist.

George had thought it odd, seeing the same man in so many different places and being ignored when he tried to address him. He'd thought it doubly odd that he only seemed to see the Man when Bill was around. He'd asked his mom about the stranger once, but when she eyed him askance and asked if he was pulling her leg, he decided to keep the matter to himself.

The Man had become an inevitability, like death and taxes. He'd frightened George as a boy; now, as an adult, George just worried he was crazy, that he was seeing someone no one else could see because no one was actually there. But the Man was such a constant fixture in his life that their encounters had, with time, become more irritating than unsettling.

Bill's head began to bob from side to side, and he let out a low moan.

"I know you're tired," said George, leaning close to his ear. "I'll get you home soon."

When they got to their car, a broken-down 2003 Chevy Malibu, George turned back to look at the gym.

The Man was gone.

2.

GEORGE DREAMED THAT NIGHT.

He wandered through an empty suburban neighborhood, trying to find his way home. But every time he turned a corner, he found himself faced with more rows of vacant houses and more empty street corners. Like a hall of mirrors, the identical buildings seemed to go on forever. Every time he turned, he would look up to read a street sign, and as soon as he continued walking, he would forget what the sign had said. He would look again, would be sure it said something different, and would already have forgotten again by the time he turned away once more.

The streets curved and stretched at odd angles, as if the world, left too long in the sun, had started to melt. The strange geometry was disorienting.

He'd grown up in this neighborhood, had spent his childhood and adolescent years here with Mom, Dad, and Bill, so why couldn't he find his way now?

As he wended through one barren street after another, he

became more and more certain he was being followed. The entity who sought George couldn't see him, he was sure of that, but it could sense his proximity, and it was homing in on him.

Meanwhile, a darkness had begun to descend over the world, not an absence of light but of substance, a hollowing in the fabric of reality. The sun lost its warmth. Colors lost their vibrancy. Reality wore down to a thin membrane, and George was scared he'd puncture it if he wasn't careful—that the whole thing would come apart like a poorly constructed stage set, revealing the true darkness beyond.

Within this darkness, George sensed he was being stalked by someone, bleeding through from another world into his own. The closer it got, the more aware of each other they became. While George moved through the warren of deserted streets, another part of himself moved in parallel through the darkness on the outside, so that he was two beings at the same time. He was George, who was running now, scrambling to get away—though he was quickly learning there was nowhere left that was safe. And he was the entity pursuing him, bubbling up through the layers of the cosmos, drawn to George like a magnet to a bar of iron.

Away. George had to get away. And outside, in the darkness, the part of himself that was this other entity caught his scent and grinned. The universe had grown ripe since it was last locked away, and it was eager to feed once more.

George turned a corner and spotted Bill leaning against a car. He knew it was Bill, even though it was like looking in a mirror; even though in real life Bill's features had long since wilted in the furnace of his disability. George's eyes fixed on Bill, so bright and full of life that George was nearly blinded.

"Bill, please, help me. I'm lost, and someone's after me."

"George?" Bill sounded surprised, as if he hadn't expected George to be there.

George felt the entity grow closer and panicked.

"Please, help me…"

It was almost on top of him now. He had to get away. George stared up at Bill a moment longer, his heart jackhammering in his chest, then took off sprinting.

"Wait, George. Come back! I have to tell you something!"

But George didn't turn, didn't stop running. That entity was right behind him, and it was hungry, and if he didn't get away, if he let it catch up to him, if he let it drag him into the dark—

GEORGE'S EYES POPPED OPEN. Terrified, he lunged for the black swivel lamp between their two beds and flipped the switch. The room exploded in harsh white light, dispelling the last vestiges of an already fading dream.

He glanced at his twin, still fast asleep, and sighed. He

was tired of having nightmares. He'd been plagued by them since childhood, ever since Bill's accident. Were the two related? George often woke in the middle of the night, feeling as if he'd been pursued and had only narrowly escaped a monstrous evil.

His arms and legs were coated in a slick film of sweat, and he peeled back the covers to air himself out. After a while, he turned out the light and closed his eyes. But the anxiety lingered, and he lay awake in bed until his alarm blared at 4:30 in the morning.

3.

A CRUMPLED BALL OF PAPER rolled across the blacktop and bounced in the wind like an urban tumbleweed. George reached for it with a mechanical trash-picker and dropped it into a large plastic bag. It was almost lunchtime, and he steeled himself for the battlefield the school would become when the bell rang.

He'd been the janitor of Walker Junior High for almost ten years. It wasn't a great living, but it almost paid the bills, and George would take any stable work he could get.

Junior high today was very different from when he'd been in school. In those days, cell phones had been rare, and teachers would confiscate them if they saw them. Now, having one was a universally accepted norm, and you were a weirdo if you didn't carry one. George could never be certain if things had changed for the better.

Rounding a corner, he spotted more trash beside a concrete flower bed and reached out to snatch it up. Through one of the classroom windows, he saw a boy with a large Afro turn from his lesson to glare at another boy in back of him, who'd just thrown a pencil at his head. George seethed when he saw the anger and frustration welling in the kid's eyes.

The kids at school used to make fun of Bill all the time, and George had fought to the last with bullies twice his size in a furious attempt to defend his brother's honor. George hoped this kid in the classroom would one day find the courage to stand up for himself—something Bill had never been able to do.

George was reaching for a dented Styrofoam cup when the Gary Jules version of "Mad World" started playing in his right overalls pocket. He set the trash-picker against a brick wall and pulled out his phone.

"Hi, Rosa. Is everything okay?"

It was Bill's current caretaker. George would have preferred to stay home and care for Bill himself, but at the roughly 10 dollars per hour In-Home Supportive Services would have paid him to do so, he would have made less than he did as a janitor. As it was, George already pictured little U.S. dollar butterflies bursting free of his bank account every time he had a bill to pay.

"Yes, I'm aware. No, I haven't forgotten."

A few weeks prior, George had come down with a terrible fever. He hadn't wanted to get Bill sick, so he'd booked a cheap room at a Motel 6 and asked Rosa to stay overnight. In-Home Supportive Services wouldn't pay her enough overtime to cover round-the-clock care, and George didn't have time to find someone else to work the hours he needed. Instead, he promised to pay Rosa for the additional time under the table, a luxury that after two days had totaled 720 dollars. He was still accumulating the meager leftovers of his paychecks after rent and utilities and hadn't yet collected the full amount.

"Rosa, I'm doing my best." A pause. "Rosa, calm down. You'll get your money."

George rubbed his forehead with the palm of his free hand.

Though the government covered most of Bill's financial burden, there was nothing they could do for the burden of time and stress in managing Bill's care. George had to fill out paperwork. He had to coordinate with a social worker. He had to keep an eye on Bill's caretakers to make sure they were doing their job— and at 10 dollars per hour, the ones he'd worked with over the years hadn't always been paragons of their profession. He'd gotten lucky with Rosa, who seemed to require little management and was good with Bill, but at some point, she, too, would move on, especially if he couldn't cough up the extra money soon.

"Rosa, I'll take care of it. I just need more time. Yes, I understand. Okay. Bye."

George ended the call and dropped the phone into his pocket.

A moment later, a burst of radio static exploded from his other overalls pocket, followed by a female voice he didn't expect—one that made all the tension in his body disappear.

"George, we've got overturned trash cans in the cafeteria. Can you take care of it?"

Already? Yet George was smiling when he reached for his thin black walkie-talkie.

"Got it, Susie. On my way."

He turned around and headed for the cafeteria.

Susie wasn't a custodian, someone George would've expected to make the call, but an administrator in the office, a pretty black-haired woman in her mid-thirties who, he'd been surprised to learn, had a crush on him. Sometimes, she would pass by where he was working, watch him lift heavy trash cans, scrub the floor in the cafeteria, or bend down to pick up wandering pieces of trash, and flash him a brief but mischievous smile. He'd thought about asking her out, but between work and Bill, his hands were always full.

He entered the building and spotted two dark gray trash cans, each stamped AUHSD for Anaheim Union High School District, turned over on their sides with milky fluids and food dribbling onto the floor. He raided a nearby cabinet for supplies, squatted beside the mess, and began to clean it up.

4.

October 1997

GEORGE, NOW TWELVE YEARS OLD, sat on the porch of his childhood home with Bill, who basked in the late afternoon sun. He'd just gotten home from Buena Park Junior High, an environment he would unwittingly reenter at Walker only a decade later. It had been George's first day back after a temporary period of home study. He'd been doing poorly in school since the accident, obsessed with Bill and consumed by guilt, and his parents had decided to pull him out for a while to give him time to adjust.

The other kids had already been talking about Bill by the time he got back, calling him names like Cripple, Fuckwit, and Retard. One of Bill's friends had come to visit, left fifteen minutes later, and hadn't been back since. It didn't take a rocket scientist to figure out where the gossip had started. The worst of it was that Bill had been fairly well liked before the accident. Now that he was different, however, everyone had turned on him, even his best friends. There was a time, George reflected with only the vague sense of shame that childhood allowed, when he, too, would have used such words. Since the accident, however, he'd learned a kinder vocabulary.

George glanced over at Bill, and for a moment he was certain he could feel the sharp, bitter sting of betrayal. But that was impossible. He hadn't told Bill about how the other kids at school had turned yet, so how could he already know?

"Let's play race car," said George, and suddenly he could feel the cloud of gloom above his brother's head evaporate.

It was a game George had invented a couple weeks ago. He would take Bill's wheelchair and zoom up and down the sidewalk. He was careful not to do it within earshot of Mom or Dad. They were still reeling from the accident and would have dragged George inside and never let him play with Bill alone again. But he knew it was something his brother enjoyed, and since the accident, he'd made it his mission to make Bill happy.

"Here we go," said George, wheeling him onto the sidewalk. "Ready?"

His twin emitted a guttural cry. A tightly wound spring inside George uncoiled and he dashed across the hot cement.

"Vuvvv!" sputtered George, his mouth vibrating like a motor. He reached the neighbor's house, turned, then made off in the other direction. "Vuvvv!"

"Hey, look! It's Retard and his brother!"

A stone fell inside George's stomach before he even turned around. Across the street stood a fat tub of lard named Scott Dunbar. He used to come over to their house on weekends to show off with his skateboard (though he'd never even landed an ollie). He'd turned out to be one of Bill's most vehement detractors.

Now, Tub of Lard flashed a predatory grin, making him look like an overly plump jack-o'-lantern. Beside Tub of Lard were two hollow-eyed posers, Greg and Ryan. They, too, had once feigned allegiance to Bill, then like Judas Iscariot had betrayed him when the political winds of the school changed direction.

"Hey!" called Tub of Lard again. "We have a question."

George closed his eyes. Clenched his fists. Opened his eyes. He inhaled. Exhaled.

In.

Out.

He'd already gotten detention and a Saturday work-study standing up for his brother, and it had only been his first day back at school. He didn't need more trouble.

"Hey, I'm talking to you," said Tub of Lard. "Or are you retarded like your brother?"

A roiling sea of anger and revulsion churned inside of George, and it was all he could do just to keep from pouncing on the little fat fuck and giving him something to cry about. He gave Tub of Lard his most menacing "don't fuck with me" glare. The two lackeys beside him shrank back a little, but that fat Cro-Magnon Scott was either too cruel or too stupid to pick up the message.

"See," continued Tub of Lard, "me, Ryan, and Greg were just wondering, how does Retard jack off when he can't use his arms?" Tub of Lard began to make small thrusting motions with his hips, to which Greg and Ryan both offered a sickening chuckle.

"Do you do it for him, George? I bet you do. I bet you—"

A jump shot in time, and then George was on top of him.

"Ow! Get off, you retard. I'll kill you, you piece of shit, I'll—"

George drew back his fist and fired.

Tub of Lard started to cry. "Stop…," he whined through a bloody nose. "Stop! Owww!"

"His name is Bill. Not Fuckwit. Not Retard. Say it."

"Say what?"

George hit him again.

"His name. Say it!"

"Owww! Bill. Billll!"

Sensing that the political winds had shifted once more, Greg and Ryan bolted.

George was about to wail on him again when he spotted the Man.

He was standing in the middle of the road, frozen like a marble statue.

Thousands of invisible mites erupted from George's skin. He was stilled, mesmerized; his eyes caught in a trap that refused to let him look elsewhere.

The Man.

George had been seeing him for a few months now, ever since the accident, and only when Bill was around. He was just beginning to figure out that nobody else could see him. Not Mom, not Dad, not his classmates. With a great many TV shows and movies under his belt about spies and law enforcement, he'd wondered at first if the Man was a secret agent following him around. Or perhaps a child predator (that possibility had kept him up at night). Now he wondered if the Man was a ghost. Did ghosts even exist? At twelve years old, he was old enough to doubt, yet young enough to still believe. Questioning the Man's very existence wouldn't occur to him until he was much older.

Then he felt Tub of Lard wriggle out from under him, just as he heard the cry from the front door of his house: "George!"

He blinked, the spell broken, and when he looked back at the street, the Man had disappeared, replaced by his mom, already barreling toward him.

George tumbled onto his side as Tub of Lard staggered to his feet.

"What's going on?" she demanded.

"He hit me!" wailed Tub of Lard, pointing at George with trembling lips.

"Get inside."

"But Mom, he was making fun of Bill. He—"

"Inside!"

George had just enough time to stare daggers at Tub of Lard before his mom smacked him across the head and sent him racing toward the house. At least, he reflected later, he'd managed to draw blood. Tub of Lard might not be very bright, but he would remember that bloody nose for a while, and if he knew what was good for him, he'd stay away from Bill.

5.

April 2017

GEORGE ARRIVED HOME a little before 3:30. He lived on the top floor of a three-story apartment complex in Anaheim, in one of the cheapest units available (though at 1,200 dollars a month, he would have hardly called it affordable). He parked in the tiny concrete garage beneath the building and climbed the stairs. There was a ramshackle elevator he took whenever he was with Bill, but when he was alone he preferred to walk.

He'd thought about stopping for lunch—he hadn't found time to eat at the school, and there was a new Mexican place down the street he'd been meaning to try—but if he didn't relieve Rosa before her hours were up, there would be hell to pay later.

He opened the front door to find her sitting on the couch beside Bill. They were watching a rerun of *Jeopardy*.

"In 1674," said the timeless Alex Trebek, "John Milton revised this epic poem into twelve books featuring God and Satan."

There was a pregnant pause, a buzzer signaling time had run out, and then Alex offered helpfully, "That famous book was *Paradise Lost*."

Rosa, a tiny woman in her fifties, was not paying attention to the screen. Instead, she focused on her latest crochet project. Bill, however, scrutinized the display as if it contained the secrets of the universe.

"Home," said George.

Rosa turned to acknowledge him before going back to the needle in her hand and the ball of yarn in her lap.

"Hello," she said, face scrunched in concentration.

"How's Bill?"

"Good." She looked up again and smiled. "Bill was very good today. No trouble, right, Bill?"

He bobbed his head in George's direction, offering him a lopsided grin.

"Well," said Rosa after a few moments, packing her things into a brown leather handbag, "I should go. See you tomorrow, Bill."

George's brother issued a rasping wordless reply.

"See you tomorrow, George."

"Bye, Rosa. Thanks."

He locked the door behind her, then sat beside his brother. There was a depth in Bill's eyes, a kind of longing that George would have given anything to fulfill. So much going on in that head of his, if only George could tap into it somehow. He talked to his brother often, sometimes into the small hours of the night, and Bill's face would always twist and convulse with frustration and understanding. Sometimes he imagined he could hear Bill inside his head, replying to his questions as well as offering insights of his own.

George watched TV with his brother in silence, through all the questions and commercials, until finally the legendary Jeopardy theme song brought the show to a close.

Then George glanced at his brother. "Ready for your walk?"

He could feel Bill's burst of excitement as if it were his own, and he didn't need to see the widening eyes to know his brother was eager.

6.

"SCOTT'S SUCH A FAT FUCK," mumbled George. He sat beside Bill's bed, a single mattress that had once been adorned with cowboy-themed bed sheets, but which now looked more like it belonged in a hospital. Bill lay with his eyes open, his head propped against a cushion, staring at George oddly through one side of his face.

George's mom had made him go to Tub of Lard's house to apologize. The smirk on Scott's face as she stood there, waiting for him to say the magic words, had ruined the rest of his day.

He'd explained to her what happened, but with a heavy sigh, she'd sat him down and told him he couldn't beat up every kid who said bad things about Bill. She said kids like Scott were insecure, that they needed to make others feel bad in order to feel good about themselves. But George wasn't buying it. Sometimes kids were just cruel, a fact many adults seemed to forget as they got older.

"I'm sorry, Bill," said George, and he didn't just mean for Scott and his lackeys. He was sorry for everything: for the car accident that had given Bill his traumatic brain injury and put him in a coma for almost three weeks, for the fact that Bill could no longer talk or move without the aid of a wheelchair, for the fact that for the rest of his life, Bill would have to be spoon-fed like a baby.

"Remember when he came over in February with his skateboard, tried to grind on the porch, and busted his lip? He cried for almost an hour. What a baby." The memory summoned the ghost of a smile. "Anyway, who cares what he thinks, right?"

And as he began to talk more, George felt a shift in the emotional current of the room, a gradual lessening of darker feelings that began to yield to an oncoming wave of amusement and fraternal love. George felt a momentum building between them, and he continued to talk about anything he could think of: about school and what it was like to be back, about all the things that annoyed him about Mom and Dad, about the injustices of twelve-year-old life and all the unrealistic burdens placed on his shoulders by parents and homework.

The irony was that he and Bill hadn't talked this much before the accident. They'd been close, of course. There was an almost mystical connection that identical twins shared, a consequence of having been forged in the same spark of life—a near telepathy that allows two people to complete each other's sentences or to know without speaking what the other is feeling. But there was another level of closeness they now shared: the kind born of shared frustration, despair, and extreme loss. With the wisdom of someone much older, George knew that, if necessary, he would offer his life in exchange for Bill's.

"You won't believe what Steve said at lunch today." Bill gazed at him expectantly. "He said they caught a guy following his little sister home from school. They arrested him, I think. Creepy."

And then George thought of the Man, and again the darker emotions surged.

"Bill, I saw him again today when we were outside. I'm scared."

Unease settled in his stomach like a worm, crawling through his midsection until he was certain the Man was waiting there in the dark behind him. If Bill hadn't been there, George would have launched from his bed like a rocket to turn on the light.

"Mom can't see him, but I know he's real. Can you see him, Bill?"

Frustration built up around the room like electricity pent up in thunder clouds. George wasn't sure if it was Bill's or his own. For a moment, the fact that Bill couldn't answer his questions really hit home, and an almost suffocating despair threatened to crush him from the inside out. The talk he and Bill were having suddenly took on a hollow cast, as if their closeness were only a sham, a construct of George's mind to protect him from soul-crushing despair.

"I don't know what to do."

Bill began to squirm like a snake, and George felt even more helpless.

"What's wrong, Bill? Are you okay?"

Bill's gyrations transformed into convulsions.

George began to cry.

"Mom!" he yelled. "Mom, something's wrong with Bill!"

It took her almost an hour to calm him down, and when George finally lay down in the bed beside Bill's, he couldn't fall sleep. A few times, he skittered across the boundary of unconsciousness, but whenever he came close to crossing it, he would feel Bill beside him, terrified and alone. George was certain he was ruminating on the Man.

When he finally got up for school the next day, his eyes were dark and bloodshot.

7.

April 2017

GEORGE PRESSED INTO the late afternoon with Bill at the fore, a crippled knight mounted on his stainless-steel steed. Somewhere in the distance, a car alarm sounded futilely. His neighborhood in Anaheim was not particularly nice, nor was it that safe, but he hadn't had any problems in the years they'd been living there. Before, they'd stayed with their mom. But once she'd passed away, it was time to move on.

A low groan emanated from Bill's throat, quiet and plaintive.

"I'm fine," said George. "Just thinking."

He wondered sometimes how he would continue to take care of his brother on a janitor's salary. Their inheritance had eased the burden some, but that source of income had almost run dry, and George didn't know what he'd do when it was gone. Maybe he and Bill could move to Arizona or Texas. Why did California have to be so expensive?

He could have finished school, could have become an accountant like his father and made much more than he was now. But he'd dropped out to help his mom take care of Bill instead. Sometimes he thought that if he'd only let her handle him a few more years, he could have taken much better care of him now. But no, Mom had already grown frail by then, had never completely recovered from Dad's death from a heart attack two years prior. As much as the loss of his degree had wounded him and made the remainder of his life almost impossible to bear, he was pretty certain it had been the right thing to do.

They rounded a corner. Standing by an abandoned bus stop was the Man. He was smoking like a chimney, peering up and down the sidewalk as if he'd lost something.

The Man often seemed to be searching for something just out of reach. George considered once more the possibility that he might be crazy. He'd had a schizophrenic aunt who used to see things no one else could see. Before she was put away, she'd tried to stab his grandmother with a kitchen knife. What if a similar transformation was about to take place inside of him?

At any rate, the Man's constant interference in George's otherwise ordinary life had gotten old, and George just wanted him to go away.

Bill groaned again.

"Are you okay? Want me to take you home?"

More groaning, an ululating plea.

Bill was frightened of something, George thought, but what? Not for the first time, George wished he knew what his brother wanted—wished there was some way for him to communicate beyond rudimentary grunts and jerky head nods. There were days he was certain he could read Bill's mind, days where an image or a thought would pop into his head unbidden and he would know for a fact it was a reflection of Bill's true desires. But there were other days when Bill's needs were a complete mystery, so incomprehensible to George that he would throw up his arms in frustration. Today was one of those days.

Exasperated because he didn't know how to make him happy, George gazed down at his brother. When he looked up again, the Man was gone.

George scratched his head for a moment. "I know, I'll make your favorite for dinner. Chicken tenders and mashed potatoes. How's that sound?"

Sometimes, when Bill was sad, George would whip up one of his favorite meals from childhood. It wasn't a foolproof strategy, yet it had been reasonably successful in the past. But the promise did little to appease Bill, and he continued to complain long after they returned home.

8.

ONCE BILL HAD TIRED of groaning, he'd descended into a soundless funk that permeated their apartment the rest of the evening. Now George sat on the couch before a silent TV, flanked on the left by his brother.

George sighed, picked a breaded chicken tender off his plate and nibbled at the edges. He'd cooked them for Bill, who'd subsequently refused to eat them.

"Sure you're not hungry?" George held a piece of chicken in front of him.

Bill shot him a dour glare. *Not hungry*, that face said. *Leave me alone.*

"Okay. More for me." But George just dropped it on the plate. "Sometimes, I think I almost understand you, but other times…" Once more, George sighed. It was no use. He'd have had better luck reading a statue.

There was a mounting tension in the air, and it was setting George on edge. He couldn't end the night like this. He had to do something, had to try and get Bill thinking of something else—anything other than what was bothering him now.

"I don't know what to do about Rosa. She keeps pestering me about the money. I told her I'm saving, that I'm going to pay her back as soon as I can, but she doesn't listen. I guess I can understand. I'd be frustrated, too."

Maybe that wasn't the best topic to discuss, given Bill's bad mood. But it had been on George's mind all day—not just Rosa but all the other money problems he had to deal with on a daily basis: food, rent, utilities, the car—and it was so natural for George to unburden himself to his brother.

"I just don't know. Now that the inheritance from Mom and Dad is almost gone, I'm not sure what's going to happen. I can't support both of us on my salary alone."

George had expected the ambiance in the room to sour further, but instead, the opposite happened. Bill's sudden concern for George was sharp and palpable. George couldn't have articulated what changed in Bill's features, but he could feel love emanate from Bill like a hot stove, cutting through whatever fog had condensed around him. Once again, they were just two brothers pitted against the world, a team in the strongest sense of the word; sharing an intense and ferocious sort of love—one that required no words, gestures, or expressions to make itself understood.

"Well," offered George, smiling a little now, "I guess I'll think of something when the time comes. We've been okay so far, haven't we?"

"Ahhg." The unexpected sound that rose from Bill's throat was a soft and tender pledge of solidarity and unconditional support.

My brother, thought George, gazing into Bill's enigmatic eyes. *Whatever happens, I'll always take care of you.* George was certain he understood.

9.

AFTER PUTTING BILL TO BED, George returned to the living room to think. So much going on. So much debt. So much stress. The weight of it all was suffocating, and so he sat there in the dark, the room's features limned in the silver light of the moon, and brooded over circumstances that were beyond his control.

Will I lose the apartment?

The car?

What will happen to Bill?

Fears and anxieties chased each other's tails through George's head. He'd never felt so helpless. Life was rarely easy, but until now, he'd managed to weather every storm and protect Bill from harm. Now George wasn't so sure things would be all right. Life, unlike the stories he used to read when he was a kid, seemed to delight in one's suffering. It was cruel, unforgiving, chaotic: a demented spectator who threw people to the lions for sport.

Pain registered in George's temples, and he leaned back with his eyes closed, waiting for it to go away.

Someday, Bill and I are going to escape all this. I'll have a nice job, a nice house, a nice car. I'll be able to pay the bills on time and focus on giving Bill the life he deserves.

But the fantasy deviated so far from reality that George was unable to enjoy it. He might as well build a spaceship and rocket himself to the moon.

George sighed, and when he opened his eyes, someone stood looking out the window with him.

The Man. Where had he come from? It was too much. Rosa, their dwindling finances, and now the Man, appearing to George in his own home in the middle of the night like a dark omen. Would he ever find peace?

"What do you want?" George's voice cut through the dark like a knife.

No reply. The Man didn't so much as twitch.

"You're always following me. I want to know why."

Still no reply.

George's face heated. "Goddammit, answer me!"

Then slowly, the Man turned.

George's veins froze. His eyes locked onto the Man's face, an indeterminate form hidden in harsh shadow, and refused to look anywhere else. George opened his mouth, suddenly dry, and tried to speak, only to realize he had no idea what to say.

The Man had acknowledged him, something that had never

happened before. It was impossible—as surreal as if time had seized before suddenly deciding to run backward. It was not the natural order of things, not the way the world was supposed to work. Only now, the rules had changed, and George had no idea what that was supposed to mean.

The apartment seemed to fade around him, as if the colors and textures of his surroundings had been sucked down a drain. The Man stood out in stark relief to the environment, and George screwed his eyes shut in terror.

"You're not real," he whispered under his breath. "Go away. You're not real."

George took a deep, shuddering breath. Held it. Hesitated. Opened his eyes.

The Man was gone.

Just like that, George's paralysis evaporated. He sprinted to the other side of the room to turn on the light—as if the Man were right behind him and would catch him if he didn't move fast enough—and trembled like a child suddenly loosed in the searing fires of Hell itself.

Not real, he thought over and over again. *Not real. Not real.*

Then another thought joined the first, an echoing counterpoint George was unable to silence.

I'm crazy.

10.

GEORGE HAD TO WORK LATE the following day. Some kid had trashed two of the bathrooms, and lucky George, he got to stay behind to clean up the mess. When he got a good look at the wads of toilet paper that clung like wasps' nests to the walls and the ceiling, and when he took in the clogged-up toilets filled nearly to the brim with brown murky water, he closed his eyes and silently prayed for eternal damnation to visit the responsible party.

He was supposed to have gone home at three. Instead, it was almost five and he was still scrubbing. Kids never thought about the guy who had to clean up after them. They were too absorbed in their shallow little worlds to give a shit.

He'd called Rosa to let her know she needed to stay longer, and once more he'd offered to pay her under the table. She balked at that, but after assuring her it would only be for two or three hours, and after doubly assuring her that he already had the money for it in his checking account and that he would stop by the ATM before he got off work, she'd reluctantly agreed.

With his bare hands, George reached into the second-to-last toilet. He felt around the smooth porcelain bottom, searching for the pulpy mass he'd found in the other units. When his fingers brushed against it, he took hold, pulled, and watched as the water spiraled down, through the drain, and out of sight.

He sighed, rose to his feet, and rinsed his hands. There was no soap in any of the dispensers, so he made a mental note to grab some from a supply closet before going home.

George couldn't stop thinking about the Man. Yesterday's encounter had stuck with him all morning and all through lunch, lending to his day a surreal and ominous quality. He was terrified of losing his grip on reality. If that happened, who would take care of Bill? And if the Man were real, what did he want? These were questions he'd managed to put off answering—questions he'd always felt more comfortable burying beneath the tedium of his daily routine where they could do little to threaten what was otherwise, aside from Bill, an ordinary life.

Bill. What did he think about all this? George had been open with him since they were kids and had included the subject in many of their late-night talks. But did Bill believe him? Deep down, George thought he might. This would have sounded crazy to anyone else, and perhaps it was just the pleading, frustrated look he could see every night in his brother's eyes, but George was sure that Bill had been trying to warn him about something. He wished desperately that they could communicate, that their late-night talks could be more than just a monologue.

George sighed and gazed back at the empty stalls. Just one more toilet to go, a last mopping of the floor, and he could finally go home.

11.

THE STREETLIGHTS HAD FLICKED on by the time George left campus, revealing a mostly empty parking lot with his own vehicle off to the side in one of the staff spaces. He stopped beneath a lamp and gazed up at the glowing orb of light. The sun had just begun to set, burning the sky in copper-colored fire that made the early evening seem even brighter. It was Friday, one of Bill's gym days, but George was too tired to go. He felt bad. Bill looked forward to swimming; it was one of his favorite things to do. But George didn't have the strength. He would relieve Rosa of her duty, spend some time with his brother in front of the TV, and go to bed.

He approached his piece-of-shit car, which he'd bought used a few years ago.

What a mistake.

It had turned out to require a ton of maintenance, nearly sending his checking account into cardiac arrest. After a while, George began to think that perhaps he should have just bitten the bullet and bought a new car. It probably would have been cheaper in the long run. There were so many financial g-forces pulling him down, slumping his shoulders, making him feel half as tall and twice as old.

When he got tired of feeling sorry for himself, he got in and started the car. He had to turn the key three times before the engine sputtered to life.

He lost himself in the steady thump of the wheels against the asphalt, and in the colors and shapes that streaked by through the side windows. Only the dimmest and most mechanical part of himself paid any attention to where he was going. The rest was somewhere far away, with Bill, with Mom before she'd died. Each recollection pointed to another more painful memory— one he didn't want to think about. It was the day everything had changed; the day Bill's and George's lives had derailed.

Every time George steered his mind in a different direction, he found it staring him in the face through the windshield once again. Every road in the landscape of his mind lead to the same place. A place of frustration. A place of pain. A place of guilt.

George had never been able to shake that. It had only sharpened over the years. He didn't think he would ever come to terms with it; didn't think he'd ever accept what had happened. Because he knew the truth.

The accident had been his fault.

12.

July 1997

"BILL?"

George stood in the doorway of his brother's hospital room, bathed in a sterile white light. His brother lay in a bed, badly bruised and unconscious. Tubes, sensors, and breathing apparatuses connected to his arms, nose, and chest. He looked like he was half machine.

George's parents were behind him. His dad laid a hand on his shoulder, communicating so many of the things he rarely expressed with words.

"Bill," whispered George, his voice hoarse, husky, and dry. "Bill, I'm so sorry. It's my fault, it's all my—" And then some mischievous creature inside George's head flipped an emotional switch, and against his will, he began to sob. He coughed and choked, gasped and sputtered, as one emotional current after another swelled and roared through him, ravaging his body; making his face hot and flushed, and his eyes painful and swollen;

45

baptizing his cheeks in the dual rivers of guilt and despair.

"George," said his mom, clutching him tight against her, beginning to cry herself. "It's okay. You didn't mean it. Nobody meant it. It was a horrible accident, a god-awful, horrible accident. Don't feel guilty, sweetie. Please don't feel guilty."

But he did. He felt the full gravity of it as it slowly crushed him alive.

They sat in a row of chairs that had been placed against the wall, and George continued to cry, pressed firmly against his mom's chest until the weight of his guilt had slowed his breathing and finally dragged him to sleep.

13.

IN THE DREAM THAT FOLLOWED, George was sitting in the same chair, only now his parents were gone and there was only Bill, lying in bed, with the same tubes and sensors connected to his face and arms. He couldn't remember what had put Bill in the hospital—only that there'd been some kind of accident, and that it had been his fault.

I did this to him.

The thought burst inside him like a grenade. The world was now a writhing sea of soul-crushing guilt. George had never before known such pain, and he felt certain the percussive force of it would kill him.

I'm sorry, Bill. I'm so sorry.

He paused, sure he could hear his brother, screaming from somewhere far away.

"Bill? Can you hear me?"

But Bill only continued to lie flat with nary a sign of life.

Yet there was some part of him that *was* with George, and with that realization, George became aware of something else.

It was there in the room with them, connecting them somehow, like one of the many cords attached to Bill's body. Only this cord wasn't something he could see; it was more like some sort of emotional umbilicus through which George sensed his brother's presence in a far-off way.

That's how I can hear him. Those are his thoughts, his dreams.

George was confident it was so, though he couldn't have said how he knew. He was also sure that connection had always been there, only he'd never noticed it before that day. But now it was getting stronger, and George could feel a tremendous power flowing from Bill into himself.

"Bill, wake up!"

From that far-off place, he thought he could hear his brother reply. But George couldn't understand what he was saying. He lunged toward his body then and began to shake him back and forth. He could hear some of the monitors connected to him begin to beep, and he could feel Bill trying to reach him. But his body remained still as a corpse, and George flew into a rage.

"Wake up, Bill!"

He was shoving him against the mattress now with such force that the bed began to shudder and rattle. Still no response, aside from that remote presence, trying to find its way back to Bill's unconscious body. And that was when George realized he had to look for him. It was the only way to bring him back.

So he can wake up.

George fled.

Now he was running through a dark, deserted corridor.

"Bill?" he called out. But there was no reply. "Bill, where are you?"

The corridor ended. Turning left, he was faced with another long hall, this time stretching toward a dark horizon.

"Bill!"

George was aware of a mounting energy flowing through their invisible bond. He could feel it working inside of him, elevating his senses so that it seemed as if his gaze alone held power over the world.

"Bill!"

"George, is that you?" The voice was still far off and faint, but a bolt of hope surged through George's heart at the sound.

"It's me, Bill. Come back!"

"I don't know how."

George imagined Bill fleeing like a frightened animal: running, reaching, searching for a way home. Only he could sense that Bill was headed in the wrong direction, and that the distance that separated them was growing every second. The cord tightened, like a bungee cable at the end of a long and perilous jump, and George, terrified their connection would snap and that Bill would be lost forever, ran after him. He let the tautness of that invisible cord lead him farther into the dark, farther into the unknown, and the hospital, soon behind him, was replaced by a black and empty void.

"Bill?"

"I'm here, George."

Still so much distance between them. The cord had almost reached its limit.

"Bill, you're too far. Come back."

A long drawn-out silence. Then, "I think I found something." The emotions flooding into George shifted from terror to curiosity.

"What is it?"

"I don't know. Maybe a way home."

George felt Bill reach out, felt every ripple and vibration it sent along that stretched-out cord. Then a sudden violent tug. George was yanked in Bill's direction like a fish caught on a lure.

"George, help!"

Bill's terror rebounded a thousandfold, and overcome now by mind-melting fear, George began to scream his brother's name.

"Bill!"

He half ran, half allowed himself to be pulled, with only one thought coursing through his mind.

Have to get to Bill. Have to bring him back.

George streaked through the darkness, the tension in the cord now doing most of the work as he rocketed forward. The world they knew was soon a million miles away, and George wondered if he was now lost like Bill.

Something came into view, something that wouldn't have made sense were George not dreaming: a thin spot in the surface of reality, like a fraying patch in an otherwise pristine pair of jeans. The cord had somehow gotten tangled inside of it, and it had started to pull against the grain, forming a slight crack through which a deeper darkness than the void had started to seep through. He could feel that Bill was stuck on the other side.

So he headed in after him.

The cord bulged and swelled, further wedging itself into the crack and opening it wider to the universe beyond, as strong emotional currents surged back and forth between them. George was terrified, but it drew his gaze and he couldn't look away.

"Help me, George!"

"I'm coming, Bill."

Pulled like a moth toward a light, he moved forward. There was a brief moment of acceleration as the crack widened to draw him in, and then he was on the other side.

Thick, tangible black. It stuck to George like tar, writhing about him like a mass of invisible insects. He turned, trying to orient himself in a world that was both impossibly narrow and impossibly wide.

What is this place?

His fear was absolute now, and it was all he could do just to remain sane. There was madness here. He could feel it as surely as he could feel the dark. It was built into the walls, into the very foundation.

And there was a presence—not his brother, but something else. Something ancient. Something evil. It had become aware of him for the first time, and George could feel its mad, delirious joy as it locked eyes with him in that far off darkness.

"Bill!"

With no sense of direction, George did the only thing he could. He followed the cord, pulling himself along its length.

Freedom, a soundless voice whispered. *Freedom*, echoed another. The feral cries that followed were like fingernails screeching across a blackboard.

When George finally spotted Bill, he was spinning in manic circles, like a dog chasing after its own tail.

"Bill, I'm here."

"This place. Oh my God, George, this place!"

"Follow me, Bill." And without waiting for an answer, George pulled up beside him, grabbed him by the arm, and yanked him back, toward the part of the cord that had gotten stuck inside the crack.

"They're the darkness," Bill whispered. "They're darkness and despair, hunger and pain. They know we're here, and they're coming for us."

We are the darkness, those silent voices agreed, and George could feel them closing in, savoring their fear. But they'd nearly reached the crack. He only had to run a little longer, a little farther…

The opening bulged once more, and George and Bill came tumbling out into an empty corridor.

The hospital. They were back in the hospital. Only now, wherever George looked, there was that crack in reality. The walls, the ceiling, the doors. He found that terrible fissure whenever he opened his eyes, the cord between him and Bill wedged inside like a garden hose stuck beneath a locked garage door. George grabbed hold of it and pulled, but no matter how much force he mustered, no matter how hard he tried to pry it free, it remained stuck. Waves of terror coursed through it like water in a pipe, and with each emotional surge, the crack opened a little wider, and the darkness leaked through a little more deeply.

"Follow me, Bill. I know the way back."

But wherever George turned, there was only another dark corridor. And at the end of it, a crack that looked out into the deeper darkness. Soon, George realized he was lost like his brother.

Bill whispered, "It's coming for us, George."

Indeed, George could feel it, too. The darkness seeping out of the walls and the ceiling had taken on physical form. A man, standing in the distance, watching with eyes that seemed to cut into George's heart like a knife.

We're coming, the Man seemed to say. *You've released us, and now we're coming.*

Then suddenly, Bill broke free of George's grasp.

"Bill, come back!"

But he'd already turned a corner and was out of sight.

"Bill! Where are you? Come back! Bi—"

14.

GEORGE WOKE WITH A SCREAM.

"Sweetie, are you okay?"

Mom. The room was dark, and her face was a pale, ghostly shadow. For a second, George almost screamed again, remembering the malicious presence from his dream. Then as she held him, the memory began to evaporate.

George cried.

"I want Bill," he said through hitching sobs.

"I do too, sweetie."

And as she held him there in the dark, as the instruments carried on with their measurements and their IV drips, Bill slumbered on, seemingly unaware.

15.

April 2017

GEORGE PULLED INTO the parking structure beneath his apartment. He shut and locked the car door, then turned and walked outside beneath an array of bright gold street lamps. The world pressed in on him from all sides, thick and suffocating, and he felt hopelessly small.

Suddenly George was sure he could feel Bill upstairs, desperate for his arrival.

George, hurry.

The thought smacked him hard and he began to stride more briskly.

He rounded the corner and nearly jumped. the Man was leaning against a car parked along the street—and he was staring straight at George. Once more, the world took on a hollow cast.

Didn't George only see him when Bill was around? Was upstairs in the apartment close enough?

Stop being crazy. The Man's not real.

57

George stopped in his tracks and swallowed.

The Man tamped a cigarette beneath one shoe. His eyes never left George.

George closed his own.

"You're not real," he whispered. "Go away, you're not real." He waited a few seconds, took a deep breath, and opened his eyes.

The Man was still there.

George backed away then and moved toward the stairs. When the Man began to creep forward, George bolted.

He took the stairs two at a time, all the while feeling the Man's sinister presence behind him, and whenever he peered over his shoulder, there was the Man, first inching toward the stairs, then slowly making his way up the steps. With each glance, the Man's surroundings dimmed further, until they were faded, dusky, and worn like a century-old photograph.

George's side was aching when he finally reached his unit. Panting, he dug through his overalls for his keys, fumbling for the one that would fit the lock. Finally finding the right one, he jammed it in and looked over his shoulder to see if the Man had caught up. As soon as the door opened, he threw himself over the threshold.

When the door slammed shut behind him, he slid down against it to catch his breath. When he opened his eyes, there was Bill, thrashing his head from side to side, and Rosa, staring at George as if he were raving mad.

16.

"GEORGE, ARE YOU ALL RIGHT?" asked Rosa.

At first, he didn't acknowledge her. The return of color and texture to George's world had dazzled his senses, reducing him to silence. After a dazed moment on the floor, he scrambled to his feet and placed an eye at the peephole, waiting for the Man to show up outside.

Behind him, Bill moaned.

"George?"

A hand on his shoulder. He recoiled from the touch before turning to find Rosa staring at him, her hand partially extended.

"What, Rosa? What?"

"Is everything okay?"

He didn't answer. He waited for the adrenaline to subside, for it to give way to weary caution. Eventually, he could feel that the Man had left, but he still opened the door a crack and peeked outside to make sure.

When he confirmed they were safe, he closed it.

"George?"

"Sorry, Rosa," he said, letting out a shaky breath. "Didn't mean to scare you. Something spooked me, that's all."

A wordless plea came from Bill. George got up and put a hand on his brother's shoulder.

"It's okay, Bill," he said. "I'm fine. Just got startled, that's all."

But Bill didn't seem placated.

Rosa had been harried, but after some time she collected herself and changed the subject.

"The money?" she asked.

"I have it." George reached for his wallet. "Here." He handed her 40 dollars: 30 for the extra hours and the rest as a tip. "Thank you very much."

She stuffed the money in her pocket, then looked up and asked, "What about the rest?"

George's forehead crinkled, and he closed his eyes. "Rosa, I told you. I'm saving up for that."

"George, I *need* the money."

"I know," he said, starting to get angry, and he had to bite his tongue to prevent himself from saying something he'd regret later. "You'll get it soon, Rosa."

She sighed and went to the couch to collect her things.

"Are you okay, Bill?" she asked, smoothing his hair.

He was rocking his head from side to side, keening softly.

"George, is he okay?"

"He's probably just tired," he said, though he could feel Bill's anxiety radiating off him like a fever. "I'll take care of him. Thanks."

"See you guys tomorrow," she said, and she left them alone in their apartment.

"What's wrong?" asked George, sitting down beside him.

Bill turned to face him, an awkward gesture that seemed to require a lot of effort. His mouth twisted and contorted as he tried unsuccessfully to form words.

George realized that Bill was worried about him.

"Hey, Bill, don't worry. I'm fine. Just a little shaken up."

He thought about mentioning the Man and what had happened outside, then decided against it. Bill didn't need more reason to be scared.

He was hoping for things to return to normal; hoping that he could go to sleep soon. But Bill was still anxious, and in the end, George had stayed up late to console him. He couldn't say when he'd fallen asleep on the couch, only that the last time he glanced at the clock, the display had read 2:16 a.m.

17.

GEORGE STOOD in an open field, the grass a deep cartoony green. He wasn't sure what he was doing there or where he was going, only that he had somewhere to be, somewhere important. His heart seized in a starburst of panic. What if he was late? What if he wandered the world forever trying to figure it out?

There was a woman sunning herself on a bench, and beside her a small plastic radio. The device tugged at his senses so that he had trouble focusing on anything else.

The radio was tuned to some far-away station with a lot of static: a dull flat *shh*. Yet every now and then, a string of words broke through.

"*Shh*...for the low price of...*shh*...call your Uncle Ben...*shh*..."

George finally managed to pull himself away and continue his journey. All the while, the sound of the radio lingered, as if the world itself were a radio.

The commercials ended and Nirvana's "Come as You Are" began to play.

Bill. He was somewhere nearby. George could feel him just beyond the range of his vision, and he stopped to look around.

He was on a highway now, on an empty stretch of road that extended beyond the horizon in both directions, surrounded by flat, rocky desert. Beside him, in the passenger seat of an abandoned car, was the same dark gray radio. The driver's-side window was rolled down.

The music continued playing.

"Bill, is that you? Where are you?"

That's why he was here, he realized, to find his brother.

"Bill?"

George strained his ears. Soon, he could pick out hidden sounds buried beneath the static. Nirvana was now interleaved with something else, a dark malevolent voice.

"Use them…kill them…"

By now, George's heart was banging out Morse code and he was having trouble breathing. He swiveled, began to turn in little semicircles as he walked up and down the road in the dry, convection-oven heat, searching for the source of the voice.

"Kill both of them…"

"Bill?" cried George.

The world had turned gray and thin, and George became aware of a looming darkness beyond.

"When we're released…Destroy…Kill…"

"Bill, where are you? Help me!"

"Coming for you…"

The owner of that voice was close, and when it got to him, it would close its hands around his throat. The world began to spin. George felt like throwing up. Meanwhile, his surroundings had dimmed to the point of near translucency, with the darkness on the outside leaching through the weakened barrier.

"Coming…Kill…"

George turned.

"Bill!"

His brother appeared before him, transfigured. He was not the broken man George had known for most of their lives, but an undistorted mirror image of himself.

"Coming for you," the voice continued. "Coming to kill…"

"Bill," said George, "we have to get out of here. He's coming."

Bill didn't speak, only stood there on the scorching asphalt, staring at him like Jesus of Nazareth. He grabbed George's shoulder, and for a moment George lost himself in Bill's eyes, wide, pleading, and wet. In that instant, the whole of Bill's mind opened to him, so full of desperation, frustration, and fear that George was nearly blinded. Then Bill pushed him down hard into the road.

Shocked, George thought he'd crack his skull. But instead, he penetrated the surface, and as he fell through endless black, the sound of the radio faded…

18.

GEORGE WOKE WITH A START to realize he'd been dozing on the couch. The clock by the TV read 4:23 a.m.

He tried to remember what had scared him and why he'd woken in a cold sweat, but like many of his nightmares, it had already slipped from his mind's grasp. All he could remember was a radio, mounting fear, and an endless expanse of black, sunbaked road.

He glanced at Bill, slumped in his wheelchair, and worried he would wake up sore if he wasn't moved soon.

He checked Bill's diaper, then wheeled him into their shared bedroom. Carefully, so as not to wake him, he unfastened Bill's straps and hefted him onto the mattress. He tucked him into his blanket, tilted his head comfortably against the pillow, checked the guardrails to make sure they were secure, and finally lay down on his own mattress.

Closing his eyes, George tried to catch some last-minute sleep. But it was no use. He couldn't shake the emotional aftershock of the dream. And so, though it was Saturday and he didn't have to go to work, he gave up and went to the kitchen to prepare a pot of coffee.

19.

SQUINTING UP AT a cluster of foliage—a jumbled mosaic of greens and browns against a backdrop of sunny blue sky—George pushed Bill's wheelchair along a winding concrete path. They were strolling through Peak Park. Ordinarily, it was another of Bill's favorite destinations, and George often took him there on weekends. But today Bill was brooding, something that was uncharacteristic for him, and George wasn't sure what he could do to snap him out of it.

Their parents used to take them to Peak Park when they were kids. Most of the other children would lunge for the playground equipment in a Texas Cage-style free-for-all, but George and Bill had always headed straight for the grass and pretended to chart unexplored worlds.

After the accident and the very long recovery that followed, George had continued to play in the park with his brother, refusing to let the fantasy die. George would take the lead by telling Bill exactly what he should see, and he was certain Bill could visualize it—that somehow his imagination had grown

71

stronger to compensate for the loss of his other faculties.

But today, George couldn't get the haunting dream of the voice and the open road out of his head. It had glommed on to his brain like glue, tainting the rest of the day.

He shivered a little, though the weather was warm.

"It's nice out, isn't it?" said George, trying to dispel the gray cloud that had settled over their heads.

Bill moaned, a sharp, inarticulate expression of profound annoyance.

"What's wrong?"

His brother's face contorted with frustration and anger.

"I wish you could tell me what was bothering you."

Bill's face grew dourer in reply.

George sighed, wheeled him to a nearby bench, and sat, wishing he could enjoy the weekend. He was usually grateful for those precious two days with Bill. It was his time to unwind, to try and forget the burdens that were always pushing down on him so hard.

"Remember when we used to play hide-and-seek?" That had been before the accident. George pointed to the grassy field nearby.

"Ahhg," replied his twin, deep and guttural.

"Bill, I don't understand why you're in such a bad mood."

His brother began to thrash his head from side to side, his face scrunched with red-hot anger.

"Hey, what's your problem?" And for the first time in a great while, he raised his voice at Bill. "Why are you being so difficult? It's not like you."

He stared at his twin, writhing as if he were frying in the electric chair.

For the past few days, he'd been getting progressively more agitated, and there wasn't any obvious reason for it. George realized he wasn't so much frustrated with his brother's behavior as he was by his own inability to understand it.

They'd developed a pretty good rapport over the years, and George usually felt he understood his brother well, certainly better than anyone else. But now, he was reminded of how little he truly knew, of all the secret thoughts that orbited around inside Bill's head, entire constellations of ideas and beliefs that they would never be able to share.

"Bill," said George, leaning in and putting a hand on his brother's shoulder. "I'm sorry. I really am. I'm trying to understand, but it's hard." A tear almost fell from his eye, but he held it back. "I just wish I knew what you wanted."

Suddenly Bill stopped thrashing. He jerked his broken face toward George's eyes, and for a moment, the two transcended the need for language, understanding each other's struggles wholly and completely.

Then the world began to dim just as Bill let out a cracked shriek.

George's head whipped around.

Sitting on the bench next to them was the Man, staring. George leaped to his feet and banged into Bill's wheelchair with a metallic clank.

The Man kept gazing at the spot where George and Bill had been sitting as if they were still there. Meanwhile, the world started to lose definition, until George felt like he was looking at the park through gauze. He imagined he could sense something more—a crack, an opening into another world, something he could almost glimpse from the corner of his eye. From it radiated a creeping darkness: thick, undulating waves that coalesced around the Man like a tornado. Whatever he appeared to be on the outside, he wasn't human.

"You can see him, can't you?" said George, putting two and two together. "That's what's been bothering you."

Bill's head bobbed up and down. Now George understood. He wasn't crazy. The Man existed. Bill could see him even if no one else could.

A dark fascination took hold of him, an unhealthy curiosity, and for a moment, time seemed to slow. The world had grown thin enough in the Man's presence that if George focused, he thought he could see part of the way through, like gazing through smoked glass. There was that crack in reality, and beyond it, the darkness. Inside were voices: a chorus of silent screams he heard not with his ears but with a sense that went beyond the physical. They were grotesque, the kind of abject horror that would stalk you during the day in every half-glimpsed shadow, that would suddenly resolve in terrifying clarity the moment you fell asleep, making you wake in a cold sweat; the kind of fear that would one day drive you into your own padded cell. And in them, through them, was the Man, expressed as a distant, staticky whisper, a sound George was certain he'd heard before in his dreams: "We're coming for you."

Finally, the Man's eyes focused on him. George nearly snapped backward. The spell was broken. The Man rose to his feet.

"Let's go!" said George, struggling as he pushed Bill across the grass.

All the while, the Man just stood there with those penetrating eyes, as if he hadn't yet registered that they were leaving. It was like being in a movie where the audio had been allowed to play out of sync with the video.

George felt like he was floating—like he was hardly there at all. The sensation of his feet as they pounded against the grass, the cries of shouting children as they jumped, climbed, and played—all of these felt hollow, as if they'd been swallowed by the darkness.

He swiveled back and forth while he ran, heart pounding, turning every so often to see the Man's eyes following his path through the park. At last, the Man seemed to process that they'd fled. A moment later, he followed briskly in their direction.

"I won't let him get you," promised George, whispering fiercely into Bill's ear. "I'll protect you."

Fingers shaking, he fished through his pockets for his keys as the Man came closer. Then he fumbled the car door open. He fiddled with the straps on Bill's wheelchair, trying to get them undone, constantly looking up to track the Man's movements.

"Almost there," George whispered, noting that the Man had nearly closed the gap. "There we go."

He hefted Bill into the front seat, folded the wheelchair, threw it into the back, and swung around to the driver's side.

"Come on," he growled when the engine wouldn't start.

The Man was about fifteen feet away.

"Start, you bastard. Fucking thing!"

Ten feet.

"Goddammit!"

The Man was almost at the door.

Finally, the engine roared to life. George backed out fast, tires screeching when he had to slam on his brakes to keep from hitting another car. He shifted gears, punched the gas, and left the Man standing in the parking lot, staring at an empty space.

20.

GEORGE SAT ON THE COUCH in their apartment, staring at a blank TV. He'd been there for at least two hours, ever since he'd returned from the park. Bright early evening light now streamed through the windows, and like King Midas, it turned everything it touched to gold.

His right leg pumped up and down like a piston, powering the gears inside his head, each grinding furiously as his brain tried to derive a solution to an ill-defined problem. George was scared. Really scared. More scared than he'd ever been in his life.

He'd put Bill to bed almost an hour ago, but he was certain his brother was awake, staring at the ceiling with that broken body of his, just as frightened as he was. Perhaps more. How helpless must he feel? George knew he could run if necessary. He had control of his arms and legs. But what about Bill? He was wholly dependent on George. He couldn't let his brother down.

At least he knew he wasn't crazy. His mind had oscillated for so long between "the Man's real" and "I'm crazy"—a maddening internal debate that had droned on and on like a presidential election—that it was a relief to finally have that question settled once and for all.

What did the Man want? He intended them harm, George was sure of that. But what was his motive? George felt as if he'd stepped into the middle of a horror movie without any advance knowledge of the script.

He wouldn't let the Man get Bill, that much was certain. But what if he got George instead? Bill didn't have anywhere to go. They had some relatives dispersed throughout various states: some elderly aunts and uncles and a few cousins, but none of them would be able or willing to care for him. He would end up a ward of the state, left to rot in some taxpayer-funded institution that would never understand him or give him the love he needed.

George had to get through this. He had to be strong for Bill.

Terror. Desperation. A dam broke inside George's head and the two emotions flooded into him, drowning all other thoughts and sensations.

Bill.

He rushed into the room to find his brother staring at the ceiling, eyes wide and bulging.

"I'm here," said George. "It's all right."

His twin had begun to thrash against the mattress, awkwardly clutching the guardrails on both ends.

"Bill," repeated George, grabbing him by the shoulders. "It's me. You're all right. Everything's going to be all right."

If only Bill could talk! If there was ever a time where talk was necessary, it was now. The bond they shared had never felt more superficial, and George fell onto the mattress beside his brother in despair.

"Bill," said George, and he couldn't help himself, not any longer. He cried, real hulking man-tears and shaking, racking sobs. All the while he clutched Bill, rocked him back and forth, cradled him in his strong muscular arms, desperate and afraid and completely out of his depth.

"I'm so sorry. I don't know what to do. I don't know how to protect you."

It was going to happen all over again, George realized, just like the accident during their summer trip to the Alamo. That had been George's fault, and if he failed to protect Bill now, this would be his fault, too.

George grabbed Bill's hand, and a powerful wave of calming sensations overwhelmed him. *Sleep*, they seemed to croon. *Sleep...* And George was suddenly drowsy.

No, have to keep my eyes open. Have to protect Bill.

But it was no use. The emotional tide was too strong, and it dragged him under.

21.

July 1997

GEORGE DREAMED. It was the same dream he'd had last night, and the night before, only just now that wasn't something he could remember.

"George, where are you?" The voice that called to him was distant, hardly more than a whisper.

He wandered down an empty hospital corridor in search of it, the only source of light the blinking LEDs of medical devices in empty hospital rooms.

"George, where are you?" Still distant, but closer. Bill. He recognized the voice now. He began to walk faster.

"Bill? Are you okay?"

He turned a corner, only to find himself faced with another dark corridor.

"George, where are you? I'm scared."

"Here," he said, becoming desperate and afraid himself. "Bill, I'm right here."

Movement, a flicker on the periphery of vision, there and gone.

"Bill, is that you?"

"I'm lost," he said, closer now. "Help me."

"I don't know where you are," George answered, running toward the sound of his brother's voice, only dimly aware that he'd already traversed a nearly infinite array of other corridors, all arranged in impossible directions.

"Keep talking," said Bill, and George thought he saw more movement, again just at the edge of his vision. "I'll follow your voice."

So George kept talking.

"Bill, I think I saw you."

"Am I close?"

"I think so. Stop moving so I can find you."

"I can't."

"Why?"

No reply.

"Why, Bill?" George rounded another corner.

Then, in a whisper that somehow carried all the way to George's ears: "He's coming."

"What?" And now George was afraid. He whirled around, and when he faced forward again, the hospital's configuration had changed once more.

"Who's coming, Bill?"

No reply.

George called out over and over again, until his throat was sore and his voice was hoarse. But Bill was gone. The world tilted and spun, and George began to trip over his own feet.

Terror. The emotion uprooted him, rearranged the structure and purpose of the dream. George was no longer running to find his brother—he was running to survive.

Another corner. Another corridor.

A crack in reality and, coming out of it, a darkness, creeping up from behind.

Another corner. Another corridor.

It was almost on top of him.

Another corner. Another corridor.

It brushed against his ear, and George thought he could hear it speak.

Another corner. Another corridor.

It reached out.

Another corner. Another corridor.

Touched his shoulder.

Another corner. Another corridor.

George screamed.

HIS EYES POPPED OPEN, and he recoiled from the hand on his shoulder.

"Relax, kiddo."

Dad? Where had he come from?

And then the dream dissolved. Bill was right there in his bed, just where he'd been when George had fallen asleep, and Mom and Dad were here, too, because he'd come with them to visit Bill in the hospital. Yes, he remembered now.

George sank to his knees, curled into himself like a roly-poly, and began to cry.

22.

April 2017

NOW, IN THE PRESENT, George dreamed again.

He was wandering down a long dark tunnel alone. On one end, a bright white light shone from a distance impossible to judge. For a fleeting instant, he was reminded of documentaries and movies he'd seen as a kid, where people who'd been clinically dead would claim they could see a light at the end of a long tunnel.

George was afraid, but he walked anyway, because he had nowhere else to go. And as he walked, the tunnel grew longer, almost as if it was alive. The walls were smooth ebony bricks illuminated by a dim but evenly spaced glow that seemed to manifest from the air itself.

He wasn't sure how long he'd been walking—it could have been a couple of minutes or a couple of hours—but he stopped when he spotted a break in the wall, the only aberration he'd seen in an otherwise uniform structure. Having something oth-

85

er than the light to follow brought him immeasurable relief. He turned toward it and continued walking.

As he moved, he observed that the walls were different, concrete instead of stone, and covered from floor to ceiling in unintelligible graffiti. It was a back alley of some sort; a dark, neglected place. At one point, it got into his head that he was searching for someone, and just as the thought occurred to him he heard a sound, distant but clear.

Crying.

It grew louder, until he was standing in front of his apartment door, only a much darker, ramshackle version of it. It didn't occur to him that he hadn't needed to climb the stairs.

George opened the door and walked inside.

The interior was in shambles. The windows were broken—some had even been boarded up—and the furniture had been tossed around as if someone had ransacked the place. Broken glass was strewn about the floor.

Sitting in the dark was Bill, gaunt and pale, huddled in his wheelchair in the middle of the living room.

"Bill?"

His brother looked up, startled.

"George?"

Bill stopped crying. Suddenly there was color in his cheeks and he'd put on weight. George couldn't have said how or when the transformation occurred, only that now, Bill looked so much like George that for an instant, he thought he was gazing in a mirror. It was Bill, but he wasn't disabled in any way.

"George?" asked Bill again. "Is that you? How did you get here?"

"Yes," he said, walking slowly toward the wheelchair. "I don't know. I heard you crying, and then I found you here."

"I never thought—" Bill stopped to wipe his nose. "I mean, I never thought you'd actually... I'm so embarrassed."

He stood and the wheelchair disappeared.

"You can walk," said George. He wasn't shocked; wasn't the least bit surprised. In this moment it felt right, as natural as breathing.

"Yes," said Bill. "I can do all kinds of things here." And for a second, despite the red puffy eyes that sparkled with newly shed tears, Bill smiled, a radiant model of emotional perfection as blinding as the sun.

Then the smile disappeared.

"George, we have to talk."

But before he could say more, the room exploded with a voice that seemed to come from everywhere at once.

"We're coming," said the voice, tinny like a radio. "We're coming for you both."

The room started to fade, and beyond, George was once more able to sense the darkness on the outside, bleeding through.

"Oh, we're going to enjoy this so much."

Bill grabbed George by the collar.

"George, don't listen. You have to—"

The voice spoke again, louder, fuller, drowning out his brother's words.

"That crippled piece of shit knows nothing. We're coming for you. We're going to kill you. Do you understand? We're going to take a knife and we're going to slit—"

George stared into Bill's eyes and, for a moment, saw entire worlds spinning just beyond their watery exteriors. Then Bill threw him down, hard, in a direction perpendicular to space and time. There was a lurch, a heave and then—

GEORGE BOLTED FROM THE MATTRESS, clutching his chest as if he'd just had a massive heart attack. This time, he managed to seize the tail end of the dream before it vanished.

He glanced around the room, filled with sinister shapes and shadows. He didn't know what time it was or how long he'd been asleep, only that it was the middle of the night.

A dream, that was all. He was worried about the Man, worried about his brother, and his brain had cobbled together the rest, a highly abstract horror film custom made for him.

George rolled over and closed his eyes, trying to steady his breathing and tamp down the dark foreboding that was causing his skin to prickle with goose bumps. He took a deep breath.

Relaxed. Teetered on the precipice of sleep.

A hand grabbed his shoulder.

George recoiled, nearly rolling over the guardrail. He turned around, and there was Bill with his eyes wide open.

"Jesus, Bill," said George. "You scared the shit out of me."

His brother moaned, soft and plaintive. His desperation was plain.

"I'm scared, too," said George. "Don't worry, we'll get through this."

Bill flailed his arms, frustrated, grabbed hold of George's shoulder once more.

"What's wrong?" He looked around, almost expecting to see the Man standing in the bedroom beside them. "Is it him? Is he here?"

Bill's head bobbed in the affirmative, and George thought he could hear a screaming voice inside his head, trying to warn him of imminent danger. A rush of liquid ice displaced the blood in his arms and legs.

"I'll look."

"Aaaarrrrgggghh!" Bill's face scrunched tight, eyes wet.

George pried himself from his surprisingly strong grip, climbed over the guardrail, and walked across the room. When he was sure no one was there, he headed for the door. Concealing himself partially at the doorway, he peeked over the threshold and took in the couch and the TV, bathed in the sinister light of nearby streetlights. He waited until he was sure the living room was empty, then walked to the bathroom.

All the while, his heart hammered in his chest. George wondered if Bill had also had a bad dream. Perhaps that was why he was so antsy. He wanted desperately to believe that.

He took hold of the bathroom doorknob. Paused. Threw the door open with a crash and flicked on the light.

The room flooded with brightness, and George squinted. When the scene before him resolved, he noted with relief that the room was empty. Letting loose a breath he hadn't known he was holding, he filled his bathroom cup with water and drank.

He stared at himself in the mirror. His hair was ragged and his eyes were red. When had life gotten so hard, so unbearable? He wanted to believe that this, too, would pass—that he would find his way through to the other side along with Bill, wherever and whatever that fabled "other side" happened to be. He wondered if there would be any relief this side of death.

He sighed, set the cup down by the sink, and turned out the light.

Exhaustion followed in the shadow of George's terror. He would sleep now. He would sink into his own pillow this time, close his eyes, and he wouldn't open them again for a long time.

He'd almost made it to the bedroom when another hand fell on his shoulder.

23.

GEORGE'S HEART STOPPED.

Time stretched.

When he turned, there was the Man, surrounded by an aura of darkness and bearing a maniacal grin.

Instinct seized control. Adrenaline surged. George drew back a fist and fired.

The experience was like nothing he'd felt before. When his hand made contact with the Man, it continued forward but slowed, as if he'd punched through thick gel. Without a solid body to absorb the blow, George staggered forward and almost fell.

Righting himself, he stared up at the malevolent specter.

Fear. Total abject fear. It dissolved his mind like acid until there was no room left for rational thought. He lunged for the bedroom, intent on protecting Bill.

"Bill!" shouted George. "He's here! Bill, he's behind me!"

His brother was already tossing and thrashing, deep primal screeches blasting from his throat.

George turned to see the Man standing at the threshold, gripping both sides of the wall. His eyes hadn't yet reached them—they were just now following George's path into the room. A few more moments and they made eye contact. The Man's smile deepened.

The Man opened his mouth to speak. The sound was faint and staticky, like that of a far-off radio station. Once more, George thought he could almost glimpse the world beyond—that he could hear those silent screams, reaching for him, urging the darker corners of his mind toward madness and despair.

George groped for the nightstand, tore the alarm clock from the wall, and chucked it in the Man's direction.

It passed through his chest slowly. The Man rippled, staggered backward. The alarm clock, having surrendered most of its momentum, sank to the floor.

The Man seemed momentarily disoriented, but after a moment, he collected himself and made his way nearer to them.

Desperate, George groped for something else. The black swivel lamp. He grabbed it and threw.

The Man was pushed back farther this time, almost into the living room, where the light bulb shattered when the lamp clattered to the floor. But his hands never left the doorway, and after a few dazed seconds, he was pressing forward again.

George thought of the rigged carnival games he'd played as a kid. Knock down a bottle, win a prize, though even a direct hit had never seemed enough to take out any of the bottles.

Finally, in a last-ditch attempt, George grabbed Bill's wheelchair. He picked it up as if it only weighed a couple pounds and threw it with all his strength.

It wasn't a direct hit. Instead, it bounced sideways off the wall with a tremendous metallic clang and moved through the Man's head.

But the Man went down, and George prayed that would be the end of it. Yet like a dark phoenix, he rose again, and George realized nothing would be enough to take him out.

"Come on, Bill," he said, and he hefted his flailing brother into his arms.

With Bill hoisted over his shoulder, he grabbed the wheelchair and dropped Bill inside. He didn't bother to fasten the straps. He rolled him out into the living room, snatched his keys, and slammed the door.

"Quiet, Bill," George said as his brother moaned and convulsed. "I'm here. Everything's going to be okay." Though George didn't know if that was true.

"Ahhg." A sad despairing sound.

George hesitated by the stairs before rerouting his brother toward the elevator. He pressed the button, hopped from one foot to the next as he waited for it to arrive, and squeezed through the doors the moment they opened. They were just closing again when the Man emerged, passing through the front door of his apartment as if it were made of water.

What is he?

A digitized ding signaled their arrival on the ground floor a few seconds later. George rolled Bill toward the car and sped off into the night.

24.

THEY STOPPED AT a Motel 6 roughly thirty miles from home. George wasn't sure how far was far enough, but it had taken the Man a few hours to return after George had driven the roughly two and a half miles to their apartment, so he hoped he had some time. He didn't want to stop. But he was exhausted, and if he didn't get to sleep soon, he thought he might cause an accident.

"Just one moment, sir," said the elderly woman at the front desk. She processed their details with agonizing slowness, stopping every so often to adjust a pair of narrow rimless glasses before continuing to tap one-fingered on an oversize keyboard that clicked and clacked like a drunk tap dancer.

Every few seconds, George would glance at the door, almost expecting the Man to follow them into the lobby. But that didn't happen, and after another five or six minutes, the woman at last handed them key cards and directed them to the third floor.

I'm not crazy, he thought as he wheeled Bill to their room for the night. *I'm not crazy. None of this makes any sense, but I know I'm not crazy.*

George was so far out of his depth that he was more than a little surprised he hadn't already drowned.

I just need some sleep. We can figure this out tomorrow.

George slid one of the two key cards through the scanner on the door, then wheeled his brother inside.

"Fuck," he mumbled when he saw the beds and realized his mistake. He'd left the guardrails at home. Well, it wasn't like he could have approached the vicious man in their room and asked nicely if he wouldn't just hold off for a moment so he could disassemble Bill's bed.

Regardless, he couldn't leave his brother in the chair. He'd develop sores. About all George could do was hold him in his arms as they slept, and hope it would be enough to prevent an accident. And speaking of accidents, without the diapers he kept in a stack by the nightstand, there was a high probability his brother would wet or shit the bed. Ordinarily, he kept a few extra pairs in the back of the car, but not today.

"Looks like we're bunkmates tonight," said George uncertainly.

He looked into his brother's eyes, and he imagined that they gleamed with a defiant light, that he could almost hear him reply.

I'll do my best not to make a mess.

Fortunately for George, when he examined the diapers Bill was already wearing, he found that they were dry. Well, there was one minor miracle in a day that was otherwise complete and total horseshit.

"Good night, Bill," said George when they were finally ready to sleep, Bill tucked tenderly under George's right arm.

I love you, thought George.

A moment later, in the stillness behind closed eyelids, a thought bubbled up in reply.

I love you, too.

25.

GEORGE STOOD IN A TUNNEL. This one was not composed of ebony bricks but of coarse, gray stone, and covered in moss, lichen, and slime. Somehow he knew this, even though everything was consumed by an almost tangible darkness. The place was strangely familiar to him, and he felt sure he'd been here before.

He stumbled forward, not sure how he could do so without bumping into the walls. There was a presence here. Something ancient. Something evil. Something that needed him. Something that wanted him to die.

This is a prison.

In the way of dreams, the knowledge came to him from on high, without pretext or justification.

From time to time, the tunnel would reverberate with a chorus of silent screams—a sensation that reminded George of nails screeching across a blackboard.

How did I get here?

Another peal of silent screams.

I have to get out of here.

He ran. Forward. Backward. He turned and spun in circles before darting off in random directions. But no matter where he went, no matter how long or how far he ran, he couldn't orient himself. He never bumped into anything, though he could feel the walls pressing in around him, tight and constricting. The very nature of this place was paradox.

We're coming…

The words were woven into the fabric of the tunnel itself. It didn't come from the darkness. It *was* the darkness. It was whoever or whatever had been locked away before time, before creation.

You're going to help us escape, and then we're going to kill you. Are you scared, George? Tell us, are you scared?

Yes, he was. This place was fear. It was fear and madness, hunger and pain. He could feel it bound up in the walls. They suffused the empty space around him, both impossibly narrow and impossibly wide.

Fear us, said the soundless voice. *This is our domain. We are darkness. We are despair. We are before all things. We are the future of all things.*

There was a weakness in the walls, George realized. A thin fissure, like a crack in a windshield. And wedged inside of it, a cord of some sort that George could feel more than see. The cord, also connected to George's side, seemed to pulse in time to the rhythm of his heart. It pushed against the crack, prying it open, and whoever or whatever was here with him was trying to break through.

The darkness grew thicker, adhering to his soul like tar, so that he couldn't breathe. His chest started to close up and he thought he might have a heart attack. In fact, for one mad moment, he was sure he would die—that he would become part of this place, food for the hungry beings who inhabited it.

Then he heard a familiar voice.

"George…," said Bill.

The sound cut through the darkness, almost tearing it down, as if it were nothing more than a cardboard prop on the set of an elementary school play.

The cord, George realized, was also connected to Bill. And if it was connected to Bill, that meant he could follow it back to him.

With only a vague sense of déjà vu, George took hold and pulled. The darkness reeled, tried to draw him back, but George kept pulling, kept letting that cord lead him away, and soon, he discovered a direction he hadn't noticed before. One kind of darkness yielded to another. There was a shift, a tug, and then—

26.

GEORGE TUMBLED INTO another tunnel, this one a construction of familiar ebony bricks. In the distance was a bright white light that once more reminded him uncomfortably of death.

"George…"

Fear and memory receded, leaving behind only a thin residue of unease that had already mostly evaporated by the time he'd turned to follow the voice once more.

There was a familiar break in the wall, and George turned and followed.

He was sure he'd been down this route before, but, nevertheless, he didn't recognize it. The passage was wide, spacious, and well lit, and lining the walls were photos of George and Bill in chronological order, from before the accident to their adult years.

At the end, on George's right, was his apartment door, slathered with a fresh coat of white paint.

"Come in," said Bill's voice. "It's open."

George tested the door and, after a brief hesitation, walked inside.

A bright flash, like a strobe.

The door opened to his parents' house, the way it used to be in the nineties, when Dad was still alive and before Bill's accident. There was their old square CRT TV, where they used to spend hours watching shows like *Ren & Stimpy*, *CatDog*, and *The Angry Beavers*. Strung up on the walls above his head were the baskets Mom had been so fond of before Dad had made her take them down. And beyond, light streamed through the sliding glass door that led to the backyard, where Dad had built a tiny fish pond when George was only five.

George had been transported back to a time when he was happy, to a life that was simple and free. He didn't want to leave.

"George," said Bill's voice.

Startled, he almost jumped. His eyes whipped around, and there was Bill, sitting on a green leather couch George hadn't seen for years.

"Bill?"

"I haven't sensed the Man yet," said his brother. "I think we're safe."

The Man.

The thought triggered something in George's brain, and his waking mind suddenly rose up from its slumber.

"I'm dreaming, aren't I?"

"Yes," said Bill. "But you and I are real. Once I realized what I could do, once I realized the connection we shared, I tried to get your attention. But either you never noticed or you never figured out that it was real."

"What connection?"

"Haven't you ever been sure you knew what I was thinking, what I was feeling, even though I haven't been able to talk since the accident? Haven't you wondered about that?"

Yes, George realized. He had. "But that's just intuition. Not like I could actually read your thoughts."

"But it's not," said Bill. He appeared to think for a moment before continuing. "I think it's something we've always shared, though I didn't notice it until after the accident. Don't you remember how we were always thinking the same thoughts, how we were always completing each other's sentences? Then it got stronger. I don't know how or why. Maybe whatever it is improved as compensation for the brain function I lost, like people who go blind often gain better hearing."

George's mind reeled with the possibility. Could Bill have been trying to communicate with him this whole time? How frustrating that must have been for him, and what a terrible missed opportunity for the both of them. But a moment later, sanity took hold once more.

"If this is a dream, doesn't that mean you're part of my imagination, too? Why should I believe anything you say?"

Bill thought for a moment, his forehead crinkling with consternation. "I'll prove it. When you wake up, ask me if the dream was real. I'll nod my head three times. How's that?"

"All right."

Bill smiled. "Okay then. Are you ready?"

"For what?"

Suddenly George's mind was assaulted by a series of loud machine-gun thoughts.

Wake up!

Wake up!

Wake up!

Blackness crept into the corners of his vision, and the dream began to fade like the conclusion of an old black-and-white film. He became aware of his body in the bed, of Bill beneath his arm. For an instant, he was suspended between two worlds. Then he opened his eyes.

George pulled away from his brother, turned onto his back, and rubbed his eyelids. Most of the dream was fuzzy now, but he could remember the end.

Ask me if the dream was real. I'll nod my head three times.

Something bumped George's shoulder. He glanced back, and there was Bill, gazing up at him with his gaunt, broken face.

George's heart skipped a beat.

It couldn't have been real.

"This is crazy," muttered George, and even after all they'd been through, he still found himself considering the possibility that he'd truly fallen off the deep end.

"Bill?" asked George, and then he stopped, teetering on the precipice of two realities. In one, the dream was real, and he'd at last discovered a way to communicate with his brother. In the other, it had just been a stupid dream, and George was about to make an ass of himself.

Could it be he feared the first possibility more than the second? There had been so many shared secrets in the dark. In the far-off realm of the imagination, George had thought Bill could hear him—that he understood all of George's deepest fears and desires. This belief had always given him some comfort. But now that he might actually find confirmation that it was true— now that Bill might at last be able to tell him what he thought— George was terrified in a way he could never have imagined. What if Bill turned out to think he was crazy? What if, after everything, Bill refused to forgive him for the accident that had crippled him?

George swallowed. Then slowly, mouth dry, he found the courage to speak.

"Bill," said George again, taking a deep breath. Beneath him, in the dark, Bill looked up with open eyes.

"Well," he asked. "Was it real? The dream? Tell me I'm not

crazy."

Minutes passed, and George was about to turn away. Then Bill's head began to move against the pillow.

He nodded.

Once.

Twice.

Three times.

George stared down at his brother.

Bill's face broke into a lopsided grin.

27.

July 1997

"GEORGE!"

Once more, he was wandering down a dark hospital corridor alone.

"Bill, where are you?" Déjà vu. In that instant, he was certain he'd asked this question before, a singular moment repeated an infinite number of times in an infinite array of possible outcomes.

A cool, sterile breeze blew past him as he moved through the dark.

"George, the Man. He's searching for us. We have to get away. Help me!"

As if summoned, George could now feel him in the distance.

"Bill," said George, "follow my voice."

"What if he finds me?"

"I'll protect you. It'll be all right. Come on."

A flicker of movement on the other side of the corridor. George ran after it, reaching the end just in time to see another flicker down the next.

"Bill, I can almost see you. Slow down."

"I'm afraid."

"It'll be all right," urged George, promulgating a confidence he didn't feel himself.

The flicker returned, resolved into the shape of a boy who was George's mirror image.

"Yes, Bill, I see you now. Stay where I can see you."

"He's coming," said his brother, looking as if he might dart off again.

George turned. There was the Man, staring in his direction with a dark grin on his face. And behind him, that crack in empty space, blacker than black—a window into a vista of unspeakable horrors.

The Man started to approach, and George darted after Bill just as Bill turned and fled around the corner.

"Bill, come back!"

The world dissolved around him, became an indistinct blur as George chased after his brother. He tried hard to keep Bill in his field of vision, the whole time sensing the Man, sneaking up from behind. the Man was only walking, yet George was certain he was gaining. It wouldn't be long before he was right on top of them.

"George…" A whisper from an empty hospital room.

He stopped.

"Bill?"

"In here."

George went inside and found his brother at last, pressed up against the door.

"George, I'm scared."

George felt his brother's fear writhe and pulse like an enraged cobra, and he clasped Bill's hand tight inside his own, unleashing a torrent of calming, soothing thoughts.

It's going to be okay, Bill. Don't be afraid. We're going to get through this. Everything's going to be okay.

A mounting wave of courage and strength surged between them, rebounding, reflecting from George to Bill and back again. Soon, George thought he could feel the darkness fade.

"Look!" Bill gasped.

George turned. Through the hospital room door came a brilliant flash of light. *The light.* They had to go toward the light. It was the way back home; the way Bill had been searching for all this time.

"Come on, Bill!" shouted George, pointing at the door, suddenly delirious with joy. "That's where we have to go! Into the light!"

"But, George, I'm scared."

"Don't be. I'll be with you."

By now, George was certain the darkness was gone, that somehow they'd driven it back.

"All right," said Bill a moment later. He bit his lower lip, but nodded resolutely. "I trust you."

George squeezed Bill's hand, and together they walked forward into the light.

28.

April 2017

A SLEDGEHAMMER OF EMOTION smashed into George's chest and he began to sob like a baby. Not only had Bill understood everything that had passed between them since the accident, he'd been trying to communicate ever since.

George thought of people in comas who could hear everything their loved ones said, yet were unable to reply.

"Bill," said George, "it was you. It was real. You can hear me. The accident, I'm sorry, I didn't mean to—"

A thought burst into George's head unbidden, so loud and so startlingly alien that he knew it wasn't his own.

I LOVE YOU.

29.

July 1997

GEORGE WOKE IN THE MIDDLE of the night to the sound of pouring rain and distant thunder. There was a sharp point in time in which he could feel his brother with him, one in which he still held his hand and knew that everything would be all right. Then the dream parted, evaporated like mist, and all he could remember was him and Bill, running for their lives through endless dark.

Outside, heavy raindrops pelted the windows. George glanced over at his brother's empty bed, and the sharp jaws of agony began to close around his chest once again. Bill still hadn't woken up. The doctors had warned it could take a while, and that every day he didn't regain consciousness, the likelihood that he ever would decreased. But he hadn't dared believe them. There was no way that could happen, not to Bill. That was the sort of thing that happened to other people—the sort of thing you read about in books, magazines, and newspapers; the sort of thing you saw in movies and on TV. George thought he'd some-how fallen asleep and was having a bad dream, only now he was trapped and couldn't wake up.

They'd stayed at the hospital for more than a day, but eventually neither he nor his parents could handle the interminable waiting. He'd felt guilty leaving his brother's side, but his parents said he needed to go back home, that it would be good for him to get some rest. He stacked that guilt on top of all the rest.

In the distance, a peal of thunder cracked and rumbled. George jumped and threw the blanket over his head.

Bill, I miss you. Come home soon.

And then, as if in reply, a thought bubbled up in the back of his head, no more than a distant whisper.

I'm here now. I'm safe.

George had begun to fall asleep when there was another crash. Startled awake, at first, he thought it had been more thunder. Then he squinted at the sudden burst of light that broke into his room and found his mom standing in the threshold, staring down at him with a rapturous smile.

"George, get up. Bill's awake!"

"What?"

"Bill's awake, sweetie. The hospital just called. They said—" And then she gazed up at the ceiling, clasped her hands and cried, "Thank you, God! Thank you!"

"They said what?" George tossed aside the covers and jumped out of bed.

His mom ran over, picked him up, and swung him in the air. It was the only time in his life he could remember her doing that.

"The doctor said Bill's prognosis is good," she said, raining down kiss after kiss on his forehead. "They don't know how far his recovery will go. They said not to get too excited, but that he's doing well so far… God, Bill's awake. My sweet boy's awake!"

"Can I see him?" asked George, suddenly overcome by a giddy, drunken hope.

"We're going now," said his mom, sweeping him into the light of the hallway. "Dad's already in the living room getting our things together."

George began to cry even before he reached downstairs. But this time, for the first time in his life that he could ever remember, they were tears of joy.

30.

MOM, DAD, DR. GAYOLES, and George huddled around Bill as if he were the quarterback of the junior high football team.

"He's only minimally conscious," explained the doctor. He waved his right hand above Bill's head, and George watched as his brother's eyes tracked the motion. "He has some awareness of his environment, but that awareness is limited and inconsistent. We're hoping for more recovery, but whether or not he'll improve, and by how much, we can't say."

"Thank you, Doctor," said Mom, and she reached out and took him into her arms. "Thank you for saving my baby's life."

The doctor smiled, allowing her to hug him for a few moments before pulling away. George guessed he'd had a lot of practice comforting patients and their families over the years.

"I have to say," Dr. Gayoles continued, "I wasn't expecting him to wake up so quickly. His brain took quite a beating. You have a strong boy. You should be proud."

Mom beamed.

119

"I'll let you and Bill have some time alone." The doctor exited the room and closed the door behind him.

"Hey, Bill," said George, leaning in close, tears brimming at the corners of his eyes. "We didn't know if you'd make it."

An overwhelming sense of love and gratitude washed over George then. If only he could hear Bill speak once more.

When he'd asked Dr. Gayoles how long it would be before Bill could talk, the doctor had explained with a guarded expression that it was best to be patient, that these things take time and that they'd know more in a few months. George got the feeling he wasn't expecting much, but after a while, he decided he didn't care.

In his childhood heart, a refuge impervious to the indifferent beatings meted out by logic and reason, he harbored a secret hope. Someday, he believed, Bill would be able to communicate. When that day came, George would be sure to tell him how sorry he was and how much he loved him.

31.

April 2017

GEORGE WASN'T SURE how long he'd been crying. It could have been all night, with Bill cradled in his arms. Now that George had learned to listen, he discovered just how active his brother's mind truly was. Thoughts that were not his own sped through his brain like cars on a freeway. They said he shouldn't feel guilty, that they'd only been kids, that he should leave the past alone and focus on the present. It was probably the first time since the accident that Bill had needed to console George.

He was only just getting used to the fact that Bill could speak to him in his dreams, and now George was discovering he could hear him even when he was awake.

All his life, Bill had been shouting from the rooftops, trying to get George's attention. All those strong intuitions of what Bill was feeling, the certainty that Bill could understand what he was saying, those hadn't just been imagination and wishful thinking. If only he'd known earlier. So many wasted years…

But his brother's thoughts were still difficult to parse individually. They came at him so much faster than language. While Bill seemed to be able to sense his thoughts just as George could sense Bill's, George found himself falling back on spoken words like a crutch. He hoped it was a skill he could develop with practice.

"Bill, it's hard. I can sort of understand you, but it's garbled. It's too much too fast."

A feeling of effort and concentration. George strained to make sense of it. Finally, some words broke through the noise.

Will try to use words.

"That helps," said George. "That helps a lot."

George found his frustration was almost more acute and painful than it had been before. They'd finally achieved two-way conversation, far beyond any of George's hopes and expectations, but it was so crude and imperfect. George felt like they'd reached the finish line only to discover it was just the first leg of the race.

An image of Bill, crumpled in his wheelchair, focusing for years on improving his brain, honing it, refining it, bulking up on gray matter, like a bodybuilder at a gym for the mind.

Takes time. Be patient.

"I'll try."

Need rest. Sleep now.

"But Bill, I want—"

Sleep.

The thought washed over him like a wave, pulling him under, making him drowsy.

George closed his eyes.

32.

GEORGE, WAKE UP! HE'S HERE!

George heard Bill whimpering even before his eyes popped open. Heart racing, he looked around. That's when he saw the Man.

He was standing by the window, sucking what little light there was out of the room. He was gazing into the night, smoking one of his goddamned cigarettes. He turned, examined George and Bill lying in bed, and smiled like he'd just spotted two very dear friends he hadn't spoken to in years.

George leaped to his feet and once more hefted Bill into his arms. The smell of shit and urine assailed his nostrils, and somewhere in the back of his mind, oddly detached, George thought, *now I'll have to change that diaper after all.* He loaded his brother into the wheelchair and backed away.

The Man's focus was sharp, and he pursued them with less delay than he had back in their apartment. He walked forward, eyes locked on George, and herded them toward a corner of the room.

George's head whipped back as he bumped against the wall, and that was when he realized there was nowhere left to run. The Man was standing so close that George could smell rotten tobacco on his breath. The screams in the darkness beyond were clear. They emphasized the hollowness of the world around them.

As George stood there like a caged animal, something inside him snapped. He'd had enough. He was through running.

"Hey," said George in a sudden rage, energy and strength flooding into his body, "leave us—"

The Man shoved him backward. Hard. He still wasn't quite solid—when his hand made contact with George's shoulder, it felt like something between the consistency of Jell-O and rubber—but the impact carried an incredible momentum that made George's head smack hard against the wall. A bright flare of pain burst inside him like a firework.

Time stopped. George couldn't speak, couldn't move. A stunned silence smothered the motel room. Up until now, the Man had only been a phantom. Now, he was something more.

George glanced down at the wheelchair beside him. Bill's eyes rolled in their sockets, and a strangled cry escaped his lips. Beneath it was a frantic singular thought that slammed into George's head like a bullet: *Don't-want-to-die!*

And that was when George realized that was exactly what would happen. The Man was finally going to finish them off, though he couldn't understand why. This was the end for both of them. The end of their love. The end of their relationship. The end of the world, as far as they were concerned.

George watched the Man's smile blossom, watched his lips unfurl like a poisonous flower to reveal sharp, bone-white teeth.

"Won't be long now," he said, the static in his voice nearly gone. "You're living on borrowed time."

Then the Man disappeared.

33.

GEORGE GLANCED AT THE DASH. Almost 4:45 a.m. He no longer had any concept of what that meant, nor how much time had passed since he and Bill had fled the hotel. It was just an arbitrary string of numbers. The gears of a great cosmic timepiece had seized, and George was suspended in perpetual terror.

Every shadow that jumped out at him through the windshield was the Man, looming, preparing to swallow them whole. George would swerve to avoid it, and only after it was in his rearview mirror would he realize it had only been a tree or a sign. He'd been honked at multiple times, but he was too exhausted to ponder the consequences of his reckless driving.

He'd burned through nearly half a tank of gas. They'd taken the 91 East until it turned into the 215 North, then merged onto I-10 East and continued on until they were as far as Redlands in San Bernardino.

Pull over.

The thought was a slap to the face. George reeled.

"What?"

Pull over.

"I can't, Bill." The Man was after them. If they stopped, they would die.

A scene popped into George's head like a 3-D movie. A sending from Bill. In it, George hovered as if he were a ghost. Their car was totaled, and a team of paramedics carried their bodies out on stretchers, covered with white, blood-laced sheets.

Pull over.

"Okay, Bill. You've made your point."

They exited on N. Eureka St., passed a Domino's Pizza, then a store called Dave's Paint N' Paper.

At that moment, the stench of Bill's soiled diaper registered again, and George momentarily came back to himself, crinkling his nose.

"You stink."

Indignation, humiliation, and fear, all in a singularity of thought.

"Sorry, Bill." George spotted a Rite Aid with its lights on and pulled into the parking lot. "I'll be right back." George opened the door.

Don't leave me!

"I'll only be gone a minute. I'll come back to change your diaper."

George's mind burst in a display of angry pyrotechnics, but

he closed the door on his brother anyway and proceeded inside.

An automatic glass door slid open as he walked in, and he imagined it was the Man's dark maw preparing to swallow him alive. Heart slamming into his chest and short of breath, he whirled. The door slid shut behind him. George raked his hair back and took a shuddering breath.

Was all this actually happening? He felt as if he'd stumbled into a movie and was almost convinced that if he veered a little to the side, he might bump into a cardboard set or knock over a camera or a microphone.

No, whispered a voice inside his head, not his brother's but his own. *This is real. You have to be strong. You have to protect Bill.*

A fresh wave of despair overtook him, and he considered that running might not do any good. Yet instinct drove him on anyway. The human spirit, thought George, was indomitable and oh so stubborn. Even when fate had already reached the finish line, the human soul continued to run, convinced in spite of everything that it could win the race.

He could still hear Bill's angry thoughts in the background and picked up his pace.

As he passed by the stationery aisle, a gleaming pair of scissors snagged his eye. Only $1.99. He stopped, reached for them, and held them up to the light. There was no way he would win against the Man with a pair of scissors. George suspected any sort of retaliation was doomed to failure. But he walked off with them anyway, feeling somehow that they might be useful.

He wandered the store in search of adult diapers, feeling out of place and out of time. When he finally located them, along with baby powder, hand sanitizer, and toilet paper, he paid a disinterested woman with green hair and a gold nose ring in cash and returned to the car.

The moment he opened the door, George was blasted by a series of telepathic invectives. He sighed.

"Bill, I'm too tired for this. Let's just go to the bathroom and get you changed. Then we can rest."

He lifted the wheelchair out of the back, struck by the unexpected weight of it. He felt like an old man now, weak not only in brawn and muscle, but in mind and character. Bill had resorted to sulking, and as George hefted him into the wheelchair, he wondered if things could possibly get any worse.

George proceeded once more to the back of the store, bag in hand. He glanced at the cashier, then entered the bathroom. Once again, he sighed.

The space was tiny and cramped, and George had a hard time juggling everything. As he pulled Bill's pants down, cringing from the smell and the mess, he could feel his brother's humiliation. Exhaustion ebbed, and he found himself empathizing. But there was nothing to do but get it over with and get out.

He threw the old diaper away, powdered Bill's hairy adult ass, and set him up with a fresh pair. Then he washed his hands in the sink, relieved to find the soap dispenser was full. He gave his hands a final slathering of hand sanitizer and wheeled Bill back to the car.

"I need to sleep," he said when his brother was once more secured in the passenger seat. "Just a couple hours."

Thank you.

George was taken aback. "For what, Bill?"

For protecting me. I'm sorry for complaining. I'm just scared.

A ghost of a smile grazed George's lips, and unexpected tears welled at the corners of his eyes. "Of course, Bill. You know I'd do anything for you."

Yes.

George didn't need to turn to see that Bill's face had broken into his characteristic lopsided smile.

George tilted his head back and closed his eyes. But before he drifted off, he thought he heard his twin, somewhere on the periphery of consciousness.

Now it's my turn to protect you.

Then he was asleep.

34.

October 1997

RUNNING.

    The Man, in pursuit.

    Bill, shouting.

    George, panting.

    Out of breath.

    The Man, closing.

    Legs, freezing.

    Bill, racing toward him.

    The Man, reaching.

    Grinning.

    Bone white teeth.

    Mouth opening.

    Closing.

    Darkness.

    Madness…

GEORGE SURGED INTO consciousness screaming.

Rivers of sweat had run down his entire body, drenching the blankets and the mattress beneath. He sat up straight, fully awake. The dream had already drained out of him, but the fear and the certainty of death had stuck by his side like a faithful lunatic bride. He jumped out of bed. Reached for the light switch. Flicked it on. The room exploded with light.

He glanced at Bill in his special bed—Mom had replaced the white sheets from the hospital with his old familiar cowboy ones just last night—and felt immeasurably relieved.

Then he noticed that Bill's eyes were open, and suddenly he felt desperately guilty. Had he woken him up? Of course he had. *Stupid*, he thought. *I'm so stupid.* The guilt that had already become a chronic condition ripped through him anew.

"Sorry, Bill," mumbled George. "Had a bad dream."

He looked into his brother's eyes and saw the struggle there, the need to communicate. *I'm here*, those eyes seemed to say. *Everything's okay now. I'm here.*

George turned out the light and tried to go back to sleep, but the shadows of unseen monsters continued to dance before his eyes. Finally, not sure what else to do, and in desperate need of comfort, he crawled into Bill's special bed, curled up beside him in a fetal position, and closed his eyes.

This time, when he fell asleep, he dreamed of Bill.

35.

April 2017

GEORGE STOOD IN A TUNNEL, surrounded by ebony bricks. Beyond, at some undefined distance, shone a blinding white light. He turned left and took a side path, where he knew he'd find Bill.

"Come in," said his twin when George reached the white door.

After a familiar flash of light, he was standing in their parents' house, where he'd first learned Bill could talk.

His brother was sitting on the couch.

"We have to talk," said Bill.

George sat on the cushion beside him.

"I'm not sure how long we have," said Bill. "I don't think he's here right now, but he could come back any time."

George looked around. Once more, nostalgia threatened to consume him. Here, in the dream, George found that his fear was muted and distant. He was lucid, fully aware of the world outside and the danger he and his brother faced. But there was also another part of him, a mental partition he didn't have access to when he was awake. It was open to him now, and it made him see things differently.

"Are you listening, George?"

"What?" He returned his attention to Bill. "Sorry, it's just—all of this is so real. It's amazing."

Bill smiled, though George could sense through their bond that the gesture was tinged with sadness, and perhaps also a touch of bitterness. "It's all I have, George. When I'm awake, I'm a broken man stuck in a wheelchair. I can't even shit without a diaper. Here, I can remember what it was like before the accident, when I could still walk, when I could do things for myself without being a burden."

Tears brimmed at the edges of George's eyes. Bill had experienced so much loss, yet at least in his sleeping hours he'd managed to create a place he could go to forget about life for a while.

But he'd been lonely, had tried for so many frustrating years to get his attention. If only he could have heard his brother's cries and joined him in this playground of the mind sooner. Well, no better time than the present.

"I've been listening to the Man's thoughts," continued Bill. "Most of them are cryptic and hard to understand, but I can pick out a few if I listen close enough. They're dark. Evil. He doesn't just want to hurt us, he wants to hurt the world. He was imprisoned a long time ago and he wants revenge."

George thought for a moment. "He could have hurt us already, but he hasn't. And I've heard him say in my dreams that I'm going to help him escape. Do you know what he meant?"

"No." Bill shook his head. "There's something he doesn't want us to know—something important. I think he knows I can sense his thoughts, and he's trying to hide them from me."

"So, what do we do?"

"I don't know," said Bill. He got up and began to pace back and forth in front of a wooden coffee table, where their dad had taught George to play chess when he was ten. "I think I'm close to figuring something out, but…I don't know."

"Do you think we can stop him? You've seen what he can do. He appears out of nowhere when we least expect him. I'm not sure if running will help."

"I don't know." Bill looked back at him, eyes alight with fear. "I'm scared, George."

"Me too. It's okay, Bill. We won't let him win. I don't know how we're going to stop him, but we'll figure something out. We can get through this if we work together."

Bill smiled then, a bright radiant grin and, just like when they were children, George decided that, if necessary, he would sacrifice his own life in order to save Bill's.

"You don't know how long I've waited for you to say something like that."

"How long have you known about the Man?" asked George. "Have you always been able to see him?"

Bill nodded. "Longer than you, I think. Do you remember the dreams we shared when I was in a coma?"

George didn't. Except suddenly he did. He'd forgotten them almost as soon as he'd woken up, but now that his subconscious was available to him again, he could remember almost every detail.

George felt his eyes widen.

"They were real," George whispered. "The dreams were real."

"Yes," said Bill. "I was trying to wake up, trying to find my way back home, only I wandered too far. And then, somehow, I got sucked into that other world. I thought I was going to die, until you jumped in and rescued me." Tears brimmed at the corners of Bill's eyes. "Even then, George, you were looking out for me."

Then a thought came to George.

"Isn't it strange how the Man has been close to us in our dreams from the very beginning, while in the real world, it seems he didn't notice us at all until just a few days ago?"

Bill's eyes flashed. "Yes, that is strange." Bill started to pace once more. "We first entered his world in our dreams, so maybe when we're asleep we're closer to him somehow, easier for him to find."

"Maybe," George agreed. "I wonder if the answer to our problem also lies in dreams."

"Perhaps." Bill looked like he was going to say more when he suddenly stopped and cocked his head toward the ceiling. "I can sense him. I hope you got enough sleep, because we have to go."

"Let's do this," said George. And a moment later, his head jerked up from the car seat.

36.

GEORGE WOKE FEELING remarkably refreshed. He was still afraid, still felt oddly detached from reality, but sleep and dreams had given him a space to organize his thoughts.

They'd driven a couple more hours, until they were somewhere in the middle of the desert on the way to Arizona. That's when he glanced at the clock on the dash and noted it was almost 9:30 a.m.

George had no idea where he was going, only that he had to drive someplace far away. He had to put as much distance between them and the Man as possible. He didn't know if it was possible, if they could truly get away, but for right now it was all he could think to do.

Every so often, he looked over at Bill, whose head was close to the open window on the passenger's side, the wind whipping over his face and hair. George felt happy thoughts flowing through Bill's mind despite his fear, and he couldn't help but feel a little uplifted.

When they were young, their parents used to take them

on road trips. Every summer, it would be the San Bernardino Mountains, or Las Vegas, or the Grand Canyon. Once, just before the accident, they'd almost made it to the Alamo. The thought conjured painful memories, and George began to brood.

Not your fault. Stop thinking about it. Words formed around a string of images that were simply there in George's mind one moment and gone the next. He turned to face Bill, whose head moved awkwardly to offer him a lopsided smile.

Don't blame yourself. We were just kids.

It was getting easier to make sense of what his brother was saying. It was like learning a foreign language. At first, it was gibberish coming at you way too fast, but if you listened long enough, the babbling coalesced into something intelligible.

"We have a lot of catching up to do," said George after a long pause. "So many wasted years. There must be so much you've wanted to tell me."

Plenty of time after this is over.

And then George began to pick up something else through their bond. Humor.

"What's so funny, Bill?"

Nothing. You're just... You don't have to talk, you know. You can use your thoughts.

George was taken aback. Yes, he supposed that was true. It just hadn't occurred to him.

Okay, thought George. *How's this?*

Too slow, admonished Bill. *Don't use words. Just thoughts. Concepts. Images. It's so much faster.*

All right.

George tried to send him something he remembered from their past, something funny his Uncle Carl had done during their ninth birthday after becoming slightly drunk.

What? Bill was confused. *You need practice. It's okay, you can use words for now.*

Embarrassed, George stopped trying. He sat there in the driver's seat, occasionally steering to stay on course, and marveled at Bill. A week ago, he wasn't even sure if Bill could understand him. Now, here he was, stronger in some ways than George, with abilities that far surpassed his own. How quickly everything had changed.

But life was like that. You were sure you had everything figured out, that you at least understood the basic outline of things, and then life shape-shifted before your eyes, transformed into something alien and unexpected.

If only the Man hadn't intervened and spoiled everything. But then again, hadn't it been the Man's incursions into their private reality that had revealed his brother's gift? If not for the Man, they might never have made contact.

"When we were young," said George, "I never expected this. I thought I'd lost you. And then you came home, and it seemed like you were aware of me. But even then, I wondered if I was just talking to myself. I tried so hard to communicate, and sometimes I was sure you were listening, that you were trying to speak yourself. But this—I never expected this."

I was trying to communicate the whole time. Sometimes I screamed and screamed inside my head, hoping you might finally hear me. But it never worked. You have no idea how frustrated I was.

"I wish I'd been a better listener."

It's not your fault, George. Sometimes we do the best we can and it's still not enough. I'm just glad we found each other.

"Me too, Bill."

37.

June 1997

TWELVE-YEAR-OLD GEORGE sat in the backseat of his dad's 1994 Dodge Dakota with Bill, who did not yet have a disability. School had let out a couple weeks ago, and to celebrate the end of their elementary school career and the beginning of their adventures in junior high, Mom and Dad had decided to take them on a road trip to the Alamo.

"You boys should see some real history," Dad had said. And now, here they were, two and a half days into their trip, and only a couple hours away from San Antonio.

"Lotta good men died there," Dad told them. "You be grateful for the freedoms you enjoy today."

And in true patriotic fashion, George and Bill had spent most of their pilgrimage through the desert pretending in turns to be General Santa Anna in hot pursuit of the Texan rebels, and Davy Crockett, the hero of their highly romanticized fantasy.

"You'll never take me alive," said Bill, whispering because

only five minutes ago, Dad had announced he was trying to drive and that they should be quiet if they didn't want a spanking.

George wrapped his hands around an invisible rifle and fired. Bill flung himself into the side of the car, as if mortally wounded.

"Dammit, if I have to tell you boys one more time to be quiet—"

"Sorry, Dad," George and Bill said in unison.

Dad grunted and continued driving. In reality, his bark was far worse than his bite, but it had usually been enough to keep George and Bill in line.

Sitting in the front passenger seat beside him, Mom rubbed his shoulder to calm him down.

"Take no prisoners," whispered George to a non-existent army, and he watched with his mind's eye as soldiers burst through the buildings inside the Alamo's walls, dragging prisoners out onto the sandy desert floor, listening to them beg for their lives before putting bullets through their skulls.

George laughed when Bill began to make outrageous faces, simulating Davy Crockett's death throes.

"Bill, you look like one of the aliens from—"

"*Mars Attacks!*" cried Bill in triumph, and they both busted up laughing.

"Boys!"

"Sorry, Dad."

Then George made a face, and Bill tittered, holding his hands over his mouth to prevent the sound from boiling over into hysterics again.

The drive had been long and tiring, but as long as George had Bill for company, he didn't think he'd ever get bored.

38.

April 2017

GEORGE AND BILL SKIPPED BREAKFAST and continued down the I-10. They'd exited California a little before 11:00, and by 12:45 p.m. they were stopping in Phoenix for gas. The already overtaxed engine of their Chevy Malibu had begun to make an ominous pinging noise, and George realized from past experience that most of the oil had burned off. He'd practically fallen on his knees then, praying he hadn't done any permanent damage to the engine.

After filling his tank and topping off the oil, George's next stop had been a sporting goods store. He didn't think a knife would do them any good, but he remembered the Man's strength when he'd slammed him against the motel room wall and decided he had to have something, if only because it would make him feel more secure.

He'd exited the store with an oversized Bowie strapped to his waist beneath his shirt, feeling like an impotent Crocodile

Dundee, and with $57.78 tacked onto an already massive credit card bill.

By now they were starving, and before hitting the road again, they made a final stop at Carl's Jr.

As George tore a Guacamole Bacon Cheeseburger into tiny morsels Bill could swallow, he ruminated on their situation. Had they won the unluckiest lottery in the world, or what?

He felt the same despondence he'd experienced after Bill's accident. Through a careless dare, he'd broken his brother, and like Humpty Dumpty, all the king's horses and all the king's men couldn't have put him back together again.

Don't give up. A thought from Bill. *We'll get through this.*

George found the encouragement strangely irritating.

"Aren't I the one who's supposed to be comforting you?"

An image of George in a big white diaper, sitting on his ass with a giant rattle, bawling his eyes out.

George chuckled. "Whatever, Bill. You're the one who wears the diaper."

Visibly, nothing changed in Bill's features. Inside, Bill went rigid. George realized he'd hurt him.

"I'm sorry, Bill. It was just a joke."

An image of Bill, mortified every time George scrunched his nose while changing him in the bathroom. An image of Bill, being spoon-fed by George like a toddler.

"Bill," said George, dropping a piece of hamburger. "I'm

sorry. It was a careless thing to say. Forgive me?"

A moment of hesitation—George could sense what went on inside his brother's head so easily now.

Okay. After that, an image of Bill holding his nose, and an image of George's sweat-soaked armpits. *I'm not the only one who smells.*

George laughed. It was true. It had been at least a day since his last shower.

After lunch, George wheeled Bill into the parking lot and checked his phone for messages.

"Oh, God." A voicemail from Rosa. She must have called while they were driving through the desert.

Somehow, the demands of life became unbearably large, even harder to face than being pursued by a murderous supernatural villain. It was ordinary life intruding on his secret world, a merging of two realities that, until now, had been separate and distinct.

George hesitated before calling her back.

"Hello?" said Rosa back in California.

"Hi, Rosa. You called?"

"George." She paused for a moment, as if surprised he'd returned her call. He heard her place something down beside her, probably another one of her stupid crochet projects. "George," she said again, "do you have my money?"

No, thought George. *Not this.*

"No, Rosa. Not yet. You know I'm try—"

"George, you keep promising, and you still haven't paid me. I need the money. If I don't get it soon, I'll have to find another job."

Irritation rose in his voice like mercury in an antique thermometer. "You'll get your money, Rosa."

"George, I want it by the end of next week. If you don't have it by then, I quit."

A dam broke inside George's head, and suddenly he couldn't give two shits what Rosa decided to do. He couldn't deal with her now, not on top of everything else. If she quit, he'd find another caretaker. He had more important things to worry about.

"Then quit."

A drawn-out pause. "George? I—"

George ended the call.

He was getting ready to load Bill into the car when he spoke inside his head.

I'm sorry.

George glanced down at his brother. "For what?"

For being a burden. For making life difficult. You could have been so much more without me.

"Bill—" George stopped to draw a ragged, hitching breath. "Bill, you're not a burden."

I am.

"You're my brother, and brothers look out for each other.

You'd do the same for me."

Bill looked up and gave him a lazy, lopsided smile, his eyes glistening in the hot desert sun.

Yes, I would.

They pulled out together, and soon they were cruising east along the I-10 once more.

39.

June 1997

"DARE YOU TO MAKE FACES at the car next to you," said Bill.

George turned toward the window.

"All right, you're on."

He stuck his tongue out, but none of the next three drivers noticed George's bold performance.

"They can't see me. You try."

Bill did, and a moment later he, too, complained he'd gone unnoticed.

They both tried over and over again, each time without success.

Then George had an idea.

"Dare you to stand up and do it."

Bill, who was on his dad's side of the car, looked down at the seatbelt around his waist, then out the window, then back at George.

"I don't know," said Bill. "Dad'll get mad."

"Come on. Don't be a wuss."

The threat had achieved its intended effect. Bill's face set with grim determination. There was a click as the seatbelt opened, a mute shuffle as Bill rose as high as the low truck top allowed, and then his face and tongue were splayed across the driver's-side window.

Dad yelled.

George grinned.

40.

April 2017

IT WAS PAST 7:00 P.M. George had been driving since they'd left Carl's Jr. a little after 1:30 that afternoon, and they were now passing through Las Cruces, New Mexico. That tap-tap-tapping noise from the engine had only started to fade a couple of hours ago, and he'd been on edge for most of the day, waiting for the lifters to throw a rod and put a premature end to their desperate journey.

He'd only stopped once for gas and snacks, and now both his tank and his stomach were once more nearing empty. He'd bought some caffeinated sodas and energy drinks during their last snack run, but they were already making negligible contributions to his ability to drive. Even when he'd bought them, he'd known the effect would only be an illusion, a desert mirage that promised alert coherence as his mind sank deeper into sleep.

Bill was also starving, though he didn't let it show on the

outside. The whole trip, he'd sat in the front seat, staring out the window as they passed one cactus or shrub after another. He tried to hide his fear, but the effort was futile; the connection between George and Bill had strengthened considerably since he'd first learned they could communicate, and there were few secrets left between them. But Bill's pride was strong, another of his faculties that had apparently compensated for the loss of his mobility, and George did his best not to shatter his brother's illusion of privacy.

At any rate, now Bill's head was slumped against the car seat, eyes closed, his mouth slack and slightly agape.

George caught glimmers of his dreams as he drove, but they were fragmented—just fleeting bits and pieces, a kaleidoscope of subconscious activity. He sensed hunger, fear, and desperation, but also love, hope, and admiration. George hoped that Bill was having more good dreams than bad.

George considered work. It wasn't his biggest concern, not now. Still, the thought had crossed his mind that he would have to explain himself before he just didn't show up on Monday. He'd left a message on the secretary's answering machine, explaining that he'd had to respond to a family emergency and that he wasn't sure when he'd be back. He had about three weeks of paid vacation. He hoped that would be enough. Maybe the Man would be gone by then.

Yeah, right. They were so screwed.

George had almost succumbed to the hypnotic rhythm of the freeway when he detected a shift in Bill's awareness, an emergence from the depths of sleep and into the shallow waters of consciousness.

"Sleep well?" asked George. He rubbed his eyes, jealous that he couldn't nod off himself. He gazed into the rearview mirror. His eyes were red and bloodshot.

No answer from Bill.

He wanted to sleep so bad, but he couldn't stop driving. He couldn't let his brother down.

Stop.

"I can't."

An image of George's head falling against the dash, of their car spinning off the road, crashing through the side rail.

Can't stay awake forever.

George needed to rest, but he also felt guilty. If Bill weren't disabled, he could take a turn driving. But he was, and so he couldn't. If George stopped, he would make them vulnerable. But Bill was right. He really did have to sleep.

"Okay, but just a couple hours."

George pulled over to the shoulder. Beside him, streams of red and yellow lights buzzed past the window.

Sleep.

He was already unconscious before his head hit the seat. And in that fraction of a second between the waking world and the world of dreams, he was dimly aware of Bill, the wheelchair-bound sentinel who stood watch beside him.

41.

GEORGE FOUND HIMSELF STANDING in a dark tunnel, surrounded by silent screams. Those screams were somehow richer, fuller than they'd been the last time he'd visited this place of fear and madness, of hunger and pain. And there was something else.

The walls were still weakening. The spiderweb-like crack he'd seen before had grown larger, fanning out in directions that didn't exist in his own four-dimensional universe. The entity bound to this place was bleeding through like moldering water, leaching into George's own world. It hadn't broken through completely, but it was close.

And that unearthly darkness hadn't just breached the barrier between worlds; it had passed through the barrier protecting George's own mind. It coursed along the emotional cord that connected him and Bill—through the same cord that was currently stuck inside that widening crack—force-feeding him insanity and fear like an infant fastened to a tainted, poisonous womb.

The cord was how the darkness remained aware of him, how it immediately shifted its focus to where George stood in the dark. Under its malevolent gaze, he took off running.

We're coming for you, George. We're going to have so much fun.

Everywhere he turned, there was the same endless black. And inside it, the Man, perpetually watching and waiting.

You can't get away from us, George. We're with you wherever you go.

Those screams pealed through his mind, a thunderstorm of hunger and rage. George wanted to claw his ears out with a knife.

Yes. That's right, George. Fear us.

The darkness swelled, crept further into his brain. Visions of the blight that inhabited this place flickered through his thoughts, turning him black with terror.

"George?"

Bill. George turned to find his brother running beside him in the dark.

"Bill, what are you doing here?"

But instead of answering, Bill just kept running. George felt his heart bang against his chest, and he started to think he wouldn't survive. His heart would burst, and when it did, he would become part of that unholy chorus, doomed to an eternity of silent screaming.

Dark visions continued to reel through his mind like a slide show. The cosmos, vibrant and bright: an ocean of stars brimming with life. Then the darkness, descending over it like an Old Testament plague: locusts devouring everything in their path, leaving in their wake an empty void that covered almost all of creation.

Then an army—immortal, blindingly bright—binding them to this prison, to the darkness outside the cosmos.

Anger. Frustration. Hunger.

Most of all, hunger. It ravaged them from the inside out, made them mad with rage. And that interminable waiting, for time without end.

The cord, thick now with thoughts that were no longer just his and Bill's, pumped him full of progressively darker images. But every time George felt he'd lose himself, Bill's spoke inside his head, guiding him back.

Stay strong, George. I don't think the Man is aware of how much he's sharing with us. We have to see as much as we can.

So George kept running, and the visions kept coming.

Hunger, reaching its climax.

Then voices, wailing in near perfect anguish.

Then a crack, a breach in the walls of their prison.

Now a human boy, lost, scrambling in the dark, with a second following on his heels.

Fear, trailing behind them, stuck inside the crack.

Stunned silence, followed by greed and hunger, followed

again by a dawning awareness of the world outside.

Fear intensifying, the crack opening wider.

A way back into the world beyond, a way to escape and feed once more.

George! I know what they want. I know why the Man's been chasing us.

Fear us, bellowed the darkness in reply. *We are the darkness, and we're coming for you. We're going to have so much fun.*

George, focus on me. Bill again. *Stay with me.*

We're coming. Nearly free, now. Nearly time to slit your throats.

Wake up, George!

We're coming…

Wake up, George!

To slit…

Wake up, George!

…Your throats.

Wake up!

Wake up!

Wake u—

42.

GEORGE SURGED INTO CONSCIOUSNESS, screaming. For a moment, he'd been suspended in a different kind of dark—the kind between sleep and the waking world—struggling to breathe, fighting to push the rest of the way through. Then he was reeling on the other side. Disoriented, his head whipped back to survey the inside of the car. When he realized he was awake, his breathing slowed.

Razor-sharp light sliced through the windshield, piercing his eyes and making him squint. He glanced at the clock on the dash: 6:15 a.m.

The light held an unearthly quality, and George found himself captivated by its mysterious nature almost against his will. He wanted to be a part of it, wanted to let it carry him into the clouds and beyond. He felt like a bird whose wings had been clipped, so that all he could do was gaze longingly toward his true home.

Then he turned and found Bill slumped against the passenger-side door, eyes open. Beside him, presumably where he'd rested his head, the window was pasted with stale drool. He looked absolutely exhausted, as if he'd just run a marathon.

George.

"You okay, Bill?"

Fine. Just tired.

George closed his eyes. That dream had been important. He tried to recall it, tried to dredge it up from the slippery depths of the subconscious.

George, I know what he wants. I know why the man's been chasing us.

The thought triggered a partial memory. Bill. He'd been there with him in the dream.

I was with you, as if his brother had heard his thought, and George supposed he had. *I saw what you saw. He didn't mean for us to see, but it got through anyway.*

"What do you mean?"

It's our fear, George. That's why he hasn't hurt us. He needs us.

"He hasn't hurt us because he wants us to be afraid?"

Yes.

"That doesn't make sense."

Frustration bubbled up from Bill like a busted sprinkler head.

It's breaking him free, George. Somehow, our fear is breaking him free.

Once more, George tried to remember. He latched on to

the only surviving image: Bill running beside him in the dark. The Man had been there, too, he realized, only he'd been more— an entire species, ancient, transcendent, powerful beyond all imagining.

And then he remembered seeing through a collective set of eyes, gazing at himself on the outside, somehow peering in, watching the crack widen before his frightened gaze.

Bill chimed in then, as if he'd only been waiting for George to make the connection.

Our fear is what's bringing him into our world.

The mental gears in George's head clicked. A circuit was now complete, and what Bill had communicated made perfect sense.

"So, we've been going about this all backwards," said George. "We've been running from him, terrified, and the whole time we've been giving him exactly what he wants." George slammed his fist into the door. "Fuck, Bill. I'm an idiot."

Not your fault. No way of knowing.

"Do you think we can stop him? Do you think if we ignore him, if we stop being afraid, we can push him back?"

I don't know.

"We should try. I thought maybe if we ran far enough, we might get away. But I don't think that's true. This might be our only way to fight back."

What if it doesn't work? What if he's already too strong?

169

"I don't know." George paused. "We need to find a place to stay for the night. We need to rest, clear our heads. No more running. Whatever happens, we make our stand now."

Like the Alamo.

"Yes," said George. "Like the Alamo."

43.

TWENTY MINUTES LATER, George and Bill drove up to another Motel 6. George pulled Bill out of the car, placed him in the wheelchair, left the knife he no longer felt he needed in the glove compartment, and locked the door. When he was done, he drew the back of his right hand across his forehead to swipe away a glistening patina of sweat.

"Seven in the morning and it's already hot."

He looked back at the freeway they'd just exited and sighed. This was it. He could feel their impending confrontation like thunderclouds rolling in over the horizon. Whatever was going to happen would happen soon.

"Bill," said George, "when this is over, if we survive—" He stopped, considered, started again. "What I mean is that we should take a road trip, maybe finally go see the Alamo. I guess we'll have to save up some money first, maybe get a new car, but—"

Yes, George. I'd like that.

Once more, he looked down at Bill, squinting against the

sunlight so that he looked a little like Clint Eastwood, and was consumed by a titanic wave of love. He waited for the emotion to pass before wheeling him up the worn asphalt path.

The room they ended up getting was small and cramped, and George couldn't believe he'd paid more than $60 for it. In the back of his mind, he knew he'd have a financial reckoning when he got home to his credit card statement. But that seemed distant right now, somehow less real, like he'd slipped through a crack in the world when he wasn't looking and ended up in a strange twilight zone where such concerns were of little to no importance. He felt strangely free, as if the Man had given him permission to worry less about the things that didn't matter.

And yet, George was also terrified.

The Man.

He wanted to believe they'd unlocked the secret to their survival, that they now possessed a talisman capable of protecting them. But he wasn't so sure. Every time he thought they might have a chance, his mind rewound to their encounter at the other Motel 6. He remembered the way the Man's hand had connected with his shoulder, how his own head had crashed into the wall, how the Man's teeth had gleamed in the darkness before him. In the face of such a concrete and dangerous interaction, the idea that ignoring the Man might somehow lead to their salvation seemed absurd.

And wondering whether he and Bill would live or die, while

freeing him from more worldly burdens, had placed an incredible pressure on his shoulders to do everything right, because who knew how much time they had left. He hoped and prayed they would come out on top, that they had years left to explore their newfound connection. But as his grandmother had been fond of saying when he was very young, "If ifs and buts were candies and nuts, we'd all have a merry Christmas."

Bill slept on the bed for most of the day, and George stayed in the room the entire afternoon to watch him. They still had no guardrail, and George needed to make sure his brother didn't injure himself.

Now, he sat at the desk, clipping coupons from a free local publication he'd found in the lobby with the scissors he'd bought in California. He didn't know if he'd actually use them, but the activity was an old habit—one born of a desperate need for survival—and it brought him comfort now.

There were ads for restaurants, car rentals, and hotels. One had even been for the Motel 6 they were staying at now. He wondered if he could apply it to the room they'd just booked. George made a mental note to ask and slipped it into his pocket with the other coupons.

George yawned. It was only a little past three, but they'd been running so hard and for so long that sleep had begun to weigh down on his eyelids like two-ton barbells.

He hesitated. He wanted to stand guard—wanted to watch

over Bill while he slept. But rest was why they were here, he reminded himself. He would be no good to anybody if he didn't get some shuteye.

So he set the scissors down on the desk and slipped into bed alongside his brother, taking him into his arms once more to prevent him from falling off the mattress. He could feel thoughts and emotions swirling through Bill's head like a cyclone and, as he drifted off to sleep, he took refuge in Bill's presence.

44.

BLACK, PALPABLE. George turned to run, but no matter where he went, no matter where he turned, it was impossible to orient himself. The walls around him resonated with thunderous peals of silent screams. They were searching for him, focusing on him, and in a moment, they would—

George.

He tried to flee, but no matter where he ran, there was that voice, always on top of him, always just on his heels.

George, why are you still trying to get away?

His heart slammed against his ribcage. Blood pounded in his ears. Escape. He had to escape.

A light caught George's eye, and he turned toward it.

Like a single burning star, it flared in the dark, pointing to a way forward.

The screams transfigured into taunting laughter and dared him to escape.

George took them up on the offer and ran. There was no way to judge how far he had to go, or in which direction he was already going, except the light grew bigger as he approached, like that of an oncoming train. All the while, those voices chittered in soundless whispers, until the light finally swallowed him whole.

Then George sat on the couch in his apartment, flipping through channels on TV. He glanced at the empty cushion beside him and was seized by a pang of heart-stopping anxiety when he realized Bill wasn't beside him. But he quickly lost focus on his surroundings and was sucked back into what was on TV almost immediately.

The screen flickered as he changed channels. News. Soap opera. Commercial. Commercial. Documentary. Commercial. News. Cooking show.

George stopped. Why did he find the cooking show so interesting? The camera focused on a light wood table, behind which a beautiful Italian vineyard shone through a broad open window. Paradoxically, the sun that shone onto the set clashed with a deeper darkness, just beyond the visible spectrum.

After a series of opening credits and an introductory jingle, the chef emerged: an odd-looking fellow, dressed in a black suit and matching fedora hat. He smoked a cigarette and looked like an extra from *The Man in the Gray Flannel Suit*. Why did he seem so familiar? The chef gazed at George through the camera and winked. The darkness centered on him, swirled around his head like a demonic halo.

"Today, we're cooking humans. Mmm," said the chef, smacking his lips. "There are so many ways to prepare them. Today, we'll explore my favorite: oven-roasted limbs."

The camera panned to follow as he walked toward the left side of the frame, where a handful of frightened preteens huddled in a cage. That was when George realized who he was.

The Man.

"I prefer my meat fresh. It's so much more tender that way." The Man dug through one of his suit pockets for a ring of keys—the large clunky kind a prison guard might have carried in an old black-and-white movie. He found the one he was looking for and sunk it into the lock with a loud metallic *thunk*.

When he recognized the kids inside, George panicked. They were all students from his school.

"Ah, this one here—" The Man approached a cowering girl with long brown curls and picked her up over his shoulder like she only weighed a couple of pounds. "This one looks nice and juicy."

The girl kicked and screamed, pounding the Man's head and shoulders.

But the Man only laughed. "Feisty, isn't she?"

"Put her down!" yelled George, but the chef didn't seem to hear him.

The camera panned back to the kitchen, where the Man held her down on a large plastic cutting board. He reached for a cleaver that hung above the stove, raised it into the air, and chopped off her right arm.

Blood gushed from the girl's shoulder like a broken water main, spattering the Man's suit and face. The girl screamed, a world-shattering howl that was no longer just on TV, but everywhere—in George's apartment, outside, beyond.

"No!" shouted George at the TV. "Don't hurt her!"

"Yes," said the Man, grinning as he cut off her remaining limbs and slit her throat, as the life poured from her jugular into a measuring cup, as her cries gave way to a sickly gurgle, followed by silence. The dark halo bulged, expanded. "Fear me. Fear makes me stronger. I told you," he said as he chucked the carcass off-camera. "You can't get away. You can run, but I'm with you wherever you go." And then he held up the nearly full measuring cup, and speaking to the audience he said, "You'll want to save the blood. It makes a wonderful sauce."

He arranged the limbs side by side in a metal cooking dish, then poured the blood from the measuring cup until it had risen close to the top. Finally, he sprinkled the dish with a pinch of salt and pepper.

"You know," he confided, "there's something else we can do to make this pop: a lovely garnish that will set things off perfectly." He walked off set once more, and when he returned, he held a boy just short of thirteen with puffy hair. George remembered seeing him in one of his classes, recalled how angry he'd been when he saw the other kids picking on him.

"You're not real!" screamed George, desperate and half mad.

"Yes," said the Man before gouging out one of the kid's eyes with a paring knife, "I am. But you already knew that."

George pulled his eyes away from the gruesome sight just as another peal of screams split the air. When he did, there was Bill, sitting beside him as if he'd been there the entire time.

Before George could react, his brother lunged toward the screen. There was an instant where George was sure the TV would shatter—that Bill would electrocute himself in a coruscating spray of glass and sparks.

"Bill, come back!"

Instead the screen bent, folded, enveloped his twin's body as if it were made of Jell-O. A moment later, he was on the set of the cooking show, facing the Man.

"Get out," said Bill.

The Man's smile disappeared. The kid, sensing an opportunity to escape, slipped from the Man's grasp and ran off-camera, clutching his empty eye socket.

"There's nothing you can do, you crippled piece of shit. I might not be strong enough to take you out yet, but I will be, and when I am—"

Bill pounced.

Static.

The image on TV morphed.

Now George was watching a boxing match, complete with a shouting commentator ticking off blows between his brother and the Man.

Bill thrust forward, jabbing at the Man's head. The Man staggered backward, the dark halo dimming, then returned fire, lunging toward Bill with a furious snarl. But Bill was too fast. He feinted, and instead of making contact with Bill's jaw, the Man tumbled onto the ground empty-handed.

Bill turned and, as soon as the Man got up, he sent a left uppercut to his chin, followed by a double right. Then he hooked the Man in the mouth, and finally landed one final jab to the Man's face.

The Man's eyes rolled up behind his head. The dark halo sputtered and vanished. A moment later, he was lying on the ground, unconscious. The referee jumped into the ring, counted down the seconds to Bill's victory, then proclaimed the match a knockout in Bill's favor.

Bill gazed through the TV, found George's eyes, and smiled.

Sleep, Bill said inside his head.

And just like that, the dream dissolved.

45.

THE ROOM WAS DARK when George opened his eyes. For a second, he thought he'd dozed on the couch in his apartment. Then he remembered the I-10 and their stop in Las Cruces, and the dream came back to him in a rush.

"Bill…" George shook his brother.

A cracked moan escaped his lips, but he didn't wake.

"Wake up." George shook him again.

Then Bill soared into consciousness like a Roman candle.

George? Is everything okay?

Bill tried and failed to turn his head. George put a hand on his shoulder to calm him.

"Fine. Everything's fine." He paused for a moment to consider what he could remember. "The dream, did that really just happen?"

And then George could tell, though his brother's head now faced the wall, that he'd broken into a broad lopsided grin.

Yes, George.

"So, that means… Bill, did you really knock him out?"

George detected elation, and perhaps also a hint of smugness.

I'm not sure what you saw—dreams aren't always how they appear on the surface—but I did manage to kick him out of your head, so you could enjoy your nap.

George realized his mouth had opened wide. He didn't think that ever happened in real life, had thought that was one of the many clichés rehashed over and over again by screenwriters and authors who didn't know how else to describe the ineffable experience of shock. Now, George could see where the trope had come from.

"Bill, how did you do that?"

By not being afraid. By standing and fighting.

Then the Man was beatable. George had never before met an obstacle he couldn't overcome until the Man. Then he'd fled, because there was nothing else he could do. He hadn't known true despair until the Man had barged into their lives. But now he was on cloud nine.

The Man was still dangerous, but he was no longer transcendental; no longer inaccessible.

George grabbed his phone, glowing white like a crystal ball, and checked the time. Only 8:30 p.m.

"Bill, we have to go out. We have to celebrate."

It's not over yet. But Bill's emotions betrayed an almost delirious optimism.

George hopped out of bed, threw the sheets aside, and swung Bill into a sitting position.

"We're going to get through this," said George.

Then he was laughing, a deep, hearty laugh. Once again, that was something he'd always believed to be a contrivance of poorly written stories, until he'd felt a great swelling relief pour out of him like caged thunder released into the wild at last. "My God, Bill, we're going to get through this."

A hoarse sound erupted from Bill's mouth, a sound George had never heard before, and he only recognized what it was through the mental bond they shared.

It was the first time since the accident that George had heard Bill laugh.

46.

June 1997

DAD, SHOUTING FOR BILL to let him drive. Mom, pleading with Bill to get down and put his seatbelt on. Bill's face, wide eyed, tongue lolling. The driver beside them, a meaty guy in a tank top with tattoos running up and down his arms, glancing up at the driver's-side window, spotting Bill and flipping him the bird.

The two brothers broke into hysterics.

It was a moment of pure joy. If George could have frozen time then, he would have. If only he'd known their lives had reached a tipping point, that things were about to get a whole lot worse.

47.

April 2017

GEORGE SAT ACROSS FROM BILL in a festive little restaurant called The Shed. It was small and sat alone in a mostly empty strip mall, but it had gotten good reviews online, and the place seemed to be packed with customers.

Bill's head jounced from side to side, taking in the colored strips of wood that hung from the ceiling like frozen salamanders. George took a bite of his fish taco and smiled.

"It's good," he said. "You try."

He cut a piece of the breaded fish with his knife and fed it directly into Bill's mouth.

Bill issued a joyful groan in the affirmative.

Relief had flooded George's veins, as if he'd been given an IV of the stuff. It felt so good not to be afraid, to have hope again. The Man hadn't occurred to him once since they'd arrived at the restaurant.

"I don't think we'll get to do any traveling for a while," said

George. "I'm using up vacation time already, and we need the money. But next year, we can take another trip, just like when we were kids."

Yes.

A teenage waitress came by to check on them. When George assured her they were fine, she refilled his root beer and left to serve other customers.

"I know I said this before," said George, staring at the tiny crystal balls of condensation that had formed around the rim of his glass, "but I really thought I'd lost you. You don't know how wonderful it is to have my brother back."

You never lost me. I was there the whole time.

"When do you think we'll see him again?" Just like that, unease nipped at his heels again.

Soon. He won't give up without a fight.

"No, I guess not." George returned his gaze to the glass. Inside, the lights above refracted through the soft drink like smoky quartz, with tiny bubbles foaming around the straw, drifting up like miniature helium balloons. "Okay," said George, as if confessing to an embarrassing truth. "I'm still a little scared."

It's okay. Be strong. We'll get through this. He wants us to be afraid. Don't give him what he wants.

"Right."

How could George have gone from feeling so confident and relieved one moment, to feeling so helpless and scared again the next? Were they just deluding themselves? Were they subconsciously trying to enjoy what little time they had left by concocting some bullshit theory that had no actual basis in reality? George was reminded of the time only a few weeks earlier, when he'd been worried he might be going crazy. Once more, the thought crossed his mind.

"Anyway, I guess whatever's going to happen is going to happen. I just want to get it over with."

George and Bill ate the rest of their meal in silence, only silence wasn't exactly the correct word. No dialogue passed between them, but a vibrant exchange of feelings and ideas flitted back and forth. Years of pent-up frustrations came bursting to the surface. Apologies were made. Pacts were agreed to. Memories were cherished. Stories were told. If George had died, he might have thought it a life in review.

Finally, after God knew how long of sitting there beneath the lights and the salamander-shaped ceiling ornaments—swimming in each other's thoughts, oblivious to the ocean of other voices around them—George glanced at his cell phone.

"It's almost eleven. We should sleep. I want to start the drive back tomorrow."

Bill agreed.

George paid, then wheeled his twin out the door, marveling at how hot the desert was even in the middle of the night.

George stared up at all the stars that spattered the celestial canvas like sparkling diamond dust and was taken aback by their vastness. He could feel Bill, also watching, pondering the age-old mysteries of time and existence, burning with questions that had mystified philosophers, theologians, and scientists for millennia.

They returned to the car in silence, their minds and hearts full, yet with so many questions left unanswered.

It wasn't until George fed his key into the ignition that he felt the sharp, cool surface of a blade push against the bottom of his throat.

48.

THE WHOLE OF TIME CONTRACTED to the size of the knife point. Despite the fact that it was dark, and that the spot where they'd parked was poorly lit, the world grew somehow darker. It was a sensation he'd grown accustomed to, and he knew who he would find even before he turned.

The Man sat behind him in the backseat, cloaked in shadow.

"Start the car," he said.

Stunned, George sat still until the Man pressed the tip of the blade into his throat, producing a bright flash of pain. Warm blood beaded on the surface of his skin.

"Start the car," the Man repeated. "If you try to get away, I'll kill you and your brother."

George believed him.

He watched people as they passed in and out of the restaurant—watched them carry on with their dull, ordinary lives—and felt a pang of jealousy.

George turned the key. The engine stalled. George turned the key again. The engine stalled once more. The knife pressed harder now, threatening to draw more blood. Desperate, George tried a third time. Suddenly, the car sputtered to life.

"Drive," said the Man. "We're going back to the motel."

George could feel that Bill was terrified, but also that he'd taken hold of himself somehow, that there was a part of him that remained composed and alert.

George, don't let the fear control you. Don't do what he says. You have to be strong.

But George *was* afraid. Aside from the fact that the Man now had a weapon, there was something different about his demeanor, a serious down-to-business attitude that chilled the blood in George's veins.

George's legs had grown wobbly, and the car juddered a couple times as he awkwardly merged back into traffic.

George, he's trying to frighten us. Don't give in.

But any time George hesitated, any time the car began to slow, the Man once more applied an upward force to the blade and promised Bill would receive equal treatment.

"I underestimated you," said the Man, turning toward Bill. "You're stronger than I thought. Too bad it won't do either of you any good." Then he turned back to George. "Ignoring me won't help. It might have, back when you first started seeing me. But I'm too strong now, too close to your world for that to hold me back."

"Who are you?" George whispered.

And then the car darkened more, if such a thing was possible. That silent, unholy chorus of screams George had heard so many times in his dreams swirled about the Man like leaves swept up in a frigid October wind, and he knew, just as he'd already somehow known, that the Man was not one but many. George caught him smiling in the rearview mirror, a pale, sickly gesture that revealed his bone-white teeth.

"We are Legion," said the Man.

George asked no more questions.

49.

"I'M GOING TO TAKE THE KNIFE AWAY," the Man said before George got out of the car. "But if you do anything other than what I say, you and your brother die."

George was like a wind-up doll, with no will of his own. He only nodded.

Don't listen to him!

George felt his face flush with shame, but he got out of the car, set up the wheelchair, and secured Bill inside it. A couple times his brother protested, thrashing against the car and his wheelchair in a futile attempt to get away. But George had already managed to buckle him in, and soon they were walking back to their room, the Man following close behind.

George had caught a glimpse of the Man's knife while in the car, and a sinking feeling had almost obliterated what little sanity remained.

It was the same knife he'd bought in Arizona—the one he'd left in the glove compartment only hours before because he thought he wouldn't need it.

Dark shadows danced across the parking lot, whispering sinister secrets, and George could feel the deeper darkness looming behind him. Shame, anger, fear: they formed an alloy of indescribable agony. In the end, when the chips were down, he'd failed to protect his brother. But what else could he have done? If he hadn't done what the Man had asked, he would have killed them both.

Except why hasn't he done that already? Doesn't that mean he still needs us? His own thought.

Yes, came Bill's unsolicited reply. *If he was ready to kill us, he would have already. That's what I've been trying to tell you.*

George stopped, transformed by the realization. Pride and adrenaline swelled within him, and he spun on the Man, standing there like a ghost beneath the light of a nearby lamp.

In what might have been the bravest moment of his life, he drew himself to his full height and said, "We're not going to do what you say anymore. You still need us. If you didn't, you would have killed us already."

The Man approached, hovering over him like a fallen angel. "Is that so?"

The black halo around him grew. Consumed the parking lot. Blotted out the lights. The world was darkness, a writhing massless void filled with unseen terrors. Those screams from beyond cried out with all their strength, and George found himself wanting to slam his face into a brick wall, or to jump off a building, anything to get rid of that awful, piercing sensation.

But he refused to be intimidated. He stood up against the darkness, and he could feel a sudden and ferocious pride erupting from Bill.

"Yes," said George, "it is. You'll have to kill us before we'll give you what you want."

But the Man only smiled, teeth blooming into a wicked Cheshire Cat grin. He stepped up to George until they were less than two inches apart, staring into his eyes, and George thought, *this is what Death looks like.*

Then the Man punched him in the face, the hardest blow he could remember. Pain exploded inside of him. Fireworks burst before his eyes, and he could taste blood in the back of his mouth.

George staggered but held his ground. He drew back his fist, ready to deliver a punch of his own. But the Man had already landed another blow, busting open his nose. Blood spurted like oil from a ruptured pipe, and he crumpled to the ground.

Get up, George! You've got this! You can take him!

George tried to move—tried to make his brother proud—but his legs were like jelly and refused to cooperate. He felt the Man reach under his arms. Smelled tobacco on the Man's breath. Struggled feebly as the Man hoisted him onto his shoulders and carried both he and his brother, along with the wheelchair, up to their room.

The Man fished through George's pocket for the key and opened the door.

"Welcome to Hell, boys."

Then he shoved them inside and closed the door.

50.

June 1997

GEORGE WAS STILL LAUGHING when Mom screamed.

"Dale, watch out!"

George's head shot up.

A car was coming, driving toward them in their lane at full speed. Dad blasted the horn and swerved to the left.

The world heaved.

51.

April 2017

GEORGE SAT ON THE BED, staring across the cramped room at the Man, who leaned against the desk. Bill was cowering in his wheelchair like a mortally wounded animal. The lights were off, and what little illumination managed to creep below the curtains was swallowed by the deeper darkness that radiated from the Man in thick, cloying waves.

George brushed the bottom of his busted lip with a finger. It had just recently stopped bleeding, and he could feel that it had swollen like a balloon.

Bill, are you okay?

Fear came to him by way of reply.

The Man stared at George, his face exposed in a broad jack-o'-lantern grin, the blade tipped toward his brother's face.

What do we do, Bill? I don't know what to do. Please, tell me what to do.

Bill's eyes rolled in their sockets.

Don't know.

Had George really felt hope an hour ago? Now, as he stared Death in the eye, it seemed a foolish, distant notion.

"Just a little longer," said the Man, breaking the silence that had settled over the room like a burial cloth.

Bill, what are we waiting for? Why hasn't he killed us? What else does he need?

I don't know!

George could feel the darkness continue to deepen, could feel the spiderweb crack he'd first sensed in his dreams continue to open. It no longer felt like they were in a motel in New Mexico, but that they'd suddenly taken up residence in a fetid underworld that only vaguely resembled the life they'd once known. It was as if the Man had not only come into their world, but that he was somehow bringing them into his own. That place was cold, black, and empty. The vacuum of space would have been more hospitable.

The Man's outward humanity seemed to be peeling away at the edges, as if he were a snake about to shed its skin. And as their world and the Man's prepared to merge in a perilous and unholy union, George could feel the voices within vibrating, writhing, eager to be free. The Man was right: Whatever he was going to do to them, he was going to do it soon.

As fear reached a climax, George felt himself part from his body, as if his mind, unable to cope with the stress, had simply torn itself in two. He retracted into himself, feeling as if he now gazed upon the world through the wrong end of a telescope. Somewhere, far away, he heard himself speak.

"Get it over with. Kill us."

"Oh, I will," said the Man. "But first, I want you to witness what you've brought into the world. Then, when we're released, when your world is ours for the taking, you can join us in the darkness. We'll have *so* much fun."

The Man began to walk around the room, the dark void trailing after him like the tail-end of a comet. And that was when George noticed something.

When the Man moved, the lamp light from outside managed to fall upon the smooth oak surface of the desk. And on that surface, George spied the pair of scissors he'd picked up along their journey, gleaming like Excalibur.

A spark of hope ignited in his heart, and he came back to himself in a brilliant flash.

Bill, look at the desk. The scissors!

He watched as Bill's eyes flicked to the right.

The Man returned, smiling. Once more, the desk and the window behind were swallowed in darkness.

I need you to distract him.

George felt his spark of hope reflected back in Bill, so that it suddenly ignited. It was a small hope, perhaps, but something left for them to try, some final way for them to make their stand.

If they couldn't win, at least they could go out fighting. If the Man was solid enough to hit him or cut him with a knife, then perhaps the Man was also vulnerable. Perhaps, if George could get ahold of the scissors, if he could plunge them into the Man's back…

"My hour arrives at last," said the Man, staring up at the ceiling. His voice was, all at once, composed of one and many—a twisted, physics-defying paradox. "A wedding feast," he mused, "between your world and ours."

And then the Man began to hum "Here Comes the Bride."

Bill, now!

George had never before seen his brother act out so violently. Bill bucked and howled, so that the wheelchair nearly tipped onto its side. Surprised, the Man turned and growled at him.

"Quiet, you crippled piece of shit!"

The Man struggled to keep him still, and the brief distraction was all George needed. He launched himself at the desk. He banged into it with a loud smack and, just as the Man spun around, George grasped the scissors in his hands and plunged them into the Man's side.

52.

TIME STOPPED. For a moment, there was only George and Bill, suspended in a perpetual moment of triumph and jubilation. After their long exodus through the desert, they'd come out victorious. They'd defeated the Man, and now they would get to make up for all those lost years.

We did it, Bill! We actually did it!

Then the darkness swelled, and George's joy shattered like a fragile stained-glass window.

He'd expected a scream, or at least a hearty *oof* as momentum and surprise forced the air from the Man's lungs. But the Man, indifferent, only gazed down at George, who was crouched before him, prostrate as if in prayer.

His reaction was so unexpected, so jarring, that George once more felt himself separate from the rest of his body.

The Man grasped the scissors and pulled them out, as bloodless and pristine as they were when George had been clipping coupons earlier that day.

"I thought you might try something like that."

The Man threw the scissors on the floor.

And that was that. They were truly out of options. George gave himself fully to the terror, frozen in position like the marble statue of a weeping angel. Meanwhile, the Man tipped his head back as if in ecstasy, drinking in George's fear like a fine wine.

"Yes," said the Man. "Fear us. The barrier between the worlds is nearly broken now."

The Man turned toward Bill, the knife still clutched firmly in his hand.

"You don't know how hungry we are, how impatient we are to feed. We tire of waiting."

This is Hell, thought George. *I'm in Hell.*

The Man turned to Bill, who in turn looked down at George as if he already knew what would happen next.

"A sacrifice," said the Man. "A lamb for the slaughter." And with that, he plunged the knife into Bill's neck.

53.

June 1997

BY CUTTING INTO THE LEFT LANE and slamming on his brakes, Dad narrowly avoided hitting the other car.

George was thrown back and to the right—a couple days later, he would require treatment for whiplash—but his seatbelt had done its job and had bound him to the seat. Bill, however, with no such restraint, slammed into the dash headfirst. The dull thud that came before he crumpled over the center console made George want to throw up.

"Bill!" George had never heard his mom scream like that before.

Bill's eyes were now closed, as if he were only asleep. George might have thought he was napping if not for the blood beginning to drip from his head.

"Bill," she cried again. "Bill, are you all right?"

She clutched his head in her hands, as if she were a female Jesus with the power to raise him up.

"Bill, say something! Bill! Dale, call 911!"

As their mom rocked Bill's broken head in her lap, scream-ing his name, willing him to heal—willing him to be all right in spite of all evidence to the contrary—their dad pushed open the door and dashed like an Olympic runner toward the nearest call box.

"Bill?" said George. He glanced over at his brother, uncon-scious and bleeding, and began to cry.

54.

FOR A MOMENT, the darkness and the Man fell away, so that, once more, there was only George and Bill; only the connection they shared, and nothing else, suspended in the timeless no-man's-land of infinity. Bill gazed down at him, blood spurting from his throat, head jerking and bobbing as the life drained out of him, and forced a weak smile.

It's okay, George. Everything's going to be okay.

Guilt. George wanted to rend his garments. The accident had been his fault, and now, in their adult years, George had failed again, this time costing Bill his life.

It's okay, repeated Bill, weakening, so many emotions flitting about as his life waned. *Not your fault. Never your fault.*

"Bill...," George whispered, tears welling in his eyes like molten diamonds.

No more pain now. Though George could feel through the bond that this was a lie.

And then as consciousness sputtered—as Bill prepared to depart from his Earthly life—George could feel something inside his head like a cord, tightening.

I love you.

The cord pulled taut. Bill closed his eyes.

"Bill!" George cried, and somewhere in the background he became aware of the Man once more, laughing, exultant.

The cord snapped. George felt that his head must have whipped back from the incredible force of it. He could feel some kind of energy drain out of him, as if he'd been unplugged from an incredible source of power. The silence in his mind was suddenly deafening; a lonely silence he'd never known before, not even when Bill had been healthy. It was complete in its isolation.

Because that connection had always been there, he realized. Maybe the accident had made it stronger, but it had always been there, only he'd never known, had never...

And now, his other half was gone.

The stronger half.

They would never make it to the Alamo. There would be no future road trips. Not now, not ever.

George was racked by violent, hitching sobs, as if he was once more only a child and Bill was once more in the hospital. But this time, he knew Bill wouldn't come home.

"Fuck you," shouted George. "Fuck you!"

"Did you enjoy the show?" cried the Man, baring his teeth. "Did you enjoy watching Retard die? Soon it'll be your turn, George, soon—"

And then the Man stopped. The knife fell to the carpet with a dull thud.

"Something's wrong," said the Man, almost to himself. "S-omething's not right. Something—"

And then he wheeled on George, livid.

"Your fear," he said through his teeth. "All this time, I thought it was your fear. But now—"

The Man erupted in a violent rage and, to George's astonishment, he'd begun to fade once more into translucency. The darkness started to recede, and that spiderweb crack started to close. The Man tried to bend down and pick up the knife, but his hands passed through it instead.

"You!" he shouted. But the sound had dimmed. It was once more staticky, as if it had been broadcast from a faraway radio station.

The Man lunged at him, and the two of them went sprawling across the floor. But there was no real substance to the Man's features anymore, only a lingering momentum that was already disappearing, even as he landed on top of George. The Man tried to hit him, tried to throttle his neck, but his hands passed through George as if he were only a shadow.

George stumbled to his feet, numb and in shock. The Man

staggered. Reeled. Stood. He turned this way and that, flailing like a madman, as if he'd gone blind and could no longer see George.

The Man was shouting, but George couldn't hear what he was saying. The Man was screaming silent invectives, fading, fading until, at last, he disappeared. That deeper darkness in the room departed with him, so that the lights from outside suddenly dazzled George's eyes, forcing him to squint.

George understood now, it hadn't just been their own fear that had allowed the Man to bleed into their world, but the connection that he and Bill had shared. It explained why George had only ever seen the Man when Bill was around. Somehow, their bond had opened that crack into the Man's prison, and now that Bill was gone, it had finally closed.

Everything ended so abruptly that George was certain he must be either mad or dreaming. He wondered if he would wake to find his brother safe in his arms in the motel room. Or better, if he would wake and find the whole thing had been a dream. Maybe, if he was lucky, the accident would never have happened at all, and George and Bill would just be two ordinary kids once more. They'd go out and play, and all that George had experienced would be abandoned behind the curtain of the subconscious.

But when George looked at the crumpled, lifeless body in the wheelchair, he knew there would be no waking from this nightmare.

"Bill…," he whispered. His brother's face was lifeless, yet the lamps outside bathed his body in a bright, angelic light.

"Bill, I tried. I'm sorry. I tried so hard—"

He wanted to cry, wanted to shout from the rooftops with his grief. But all those agonizing emotions had backed up somehow, so that the barren wasteland of shock dried his eyes and stilled his frantically beating heart.

He got up and walked over to the wheelchair, to his brother's blood-spattered body. He reached out and put his fingers into Bill's hair, as if to confirm that he was indeed deceased, that some cosmic spark wouldn't suddenly restart his failed heart.

"I love you," said George, a pure and simple fact. And then he was walking toward the door, devoid of emotion.

He stepped outside into the warm desert air and stared at the I-10 in the distance. Then all at once, everything that had happened fell on his shoulders in a crippling heap. Screaming, he ran toward the office to call 911. The whole time, Bill's noble visage remained before his eyes, fixed forever in his vision like a guiding star.

55.

May 2017

GEORGE CRUISED DOWN THE I-10 WEST at a steady 80 miles per hour, headed back to California. He'd left Las Cruces while it was still dark. Now he was only a couple hours from Phoenix, and the sun was a sparkling starburst across the windshield. The heavy weight of silence sat upon his shoulders, a weight he'd just started to grow accustomed to in the last two and a half weeks.

He'd never before realized how utterly alone one could feel. It had been painful at first, then draining—a perpetual black hole that seemed always to hover over his shoulder. He did not cry, not because he wasn't crushed, but because, like the ancient riverbeds in the desert he'd just emerged from, the tear ducts of his eyes had dried. Was loneliness like that for everyone? Was that why so many people overdosed on drugs or drowned themselves in alcohol rather than face the prospect of living alone?

At least he'd been allowed to go home. There was that small

blessing.

He'd been detained by the police, something that in retrospect he thought he should have seen coming from a mile away. They'd found the bloody knife on the motel room floor with only his fingerprints alongside Bill's broken, bled-out body, and they'd come to the only logical conclusion possible. At the time, George hadn't been able to muster the energy to protest. He'd been too shocked by Bill's death to understand what was happening. He'd let them cuff him, fingerprint him, and interrogate him in stoic, absent silence.

Fortunately, CCTV footage from the motel's parking lot had surfaced, showing the Man getting out of the car with George and Bill, as well as holding the knife and knocking George out, then carrying both he and his brother up the stairs.

George had come alive only after seeing that. He'd tried to flee, and someone had had to restrain him and calm him down.

He wondered later why the camera had been able to capture the Man's visage when nobody had seen him before. Perhaps as the Man got more solid and defined, as he came more fully into the world, other people and things would have started to register his presence as well.

The police wanted to know what the struggle was about, but George hadn't been able to provide a satisfactory answer. In the end, they held him long enough to decide it wasn't him who killed his brother. After they pumped him for whatever information he could provide, they let him go. They said they'd send the body home, so George could have a funeral, and then George prepared for the long drive home in silence.

He could see the rest of his life, fanned out before him in a dark and uncertain horizon. His purpose had always been centered on Bill and his needs. Now that he had to look out for himself, he was anxious and afraid. What was the meaning of life after Bill?

Each landmark along the way transformed into a monument he knew would be forever carved into the surface of his heart. Every time he passed one—a gas station here, a fast-food place there—he would reach out to Bill and ask for help. Where should he go from here? What should he do when he got home? Even from the hereafter, it seemed that if George listened patiently enough, perhaps Bill might speak.

But for the rest of the trip home, his brother remained frustratingly and perplexingly silent.

56.

September 2017

SUSIE SMILED, and George's heart skipped a beat. He would have thought that was a feeling reserved for pimple-faced preteens, but it seemed some things didn't change with age.

They were sitting together in the staff lounge, eating lunch. Someone was covering for him while he took his break, but he had less than fifteen minutes before he had to get back to work. He had to act fast.

In between bites of pepperoni pizza, George regaled her with lurid tales of janitorial horrors. She seemed to laugh in all the right places, and he felt his cheeks burn a bright cherry red.

He had no idea what to do. He'd asked a few girls out in high school, but most of his adult life had been spent with Bill. It was not a subject he was well versed in, and now he was certain his inexperience was showing. Yet he soldiered on. He thought this was something Bill would have wanted.

"That sounds terrible," she said. "Is it like that every day?"

"No," said George, just managing to keep his voice level. "Not every day. Saturday and Sunday are usually fine."

She giggled. "Kids can be little shits."

Caught off guard by the candid statement, George laughed in earnest.

It was strange, this exchange of words between two physically healthy people. It was something George had experienced so little of beyond business and pleasantries. What he'd shared with Bill had been far more immediate, intimate, and revealing. Was the same level of intimacy possible without that strange mental connection? George didn't know, but he thought he'd like to find out.

He glanced at his watch. Twelve minutes left. Time to get in the game or go home.

"Susie…"

His palms were clammy and slick with a fresh coat of sweat. He took a deep breath before continuing.

"I was thinking, if you're not busy—" He was fumbling like a blind man without his cane. "There's a nice place in Fullerton, The Vine."

He'd never been there before and didn't know if it was actually nice. He'd just looked it up online and hoped for the best. The pictures and menu he'd seen along with the reviews suggested the place might be expensive, but because he was only supporting himself now, he'd finally made some progress on his bills and could afford to spend a little extra.

"If you want to kick back after work, swap horror stories…"

She looked up at him, and for a moment he saw two possible outcomes—each equally as likely—hovering before him in a terrifying cloud of probabilities. Then she flashed him an inviting smile that made his heart leap.

"Sure. It would be nice to swap war stories with a fellow veteran."

George let loose a breath he hadn't realized he was holding. Susie must have noticed, but if she had, she didn't let on.

"Great," he said, smiling himself now. "How about eight?"

Other Books by Jeff Coleman

Dying Breath, a short story (e-book)
Rite of Passage, a short story (e-book and hardcover)
Snapshots: The Collected Flash Fiction of Jeff Coleman, Volume 1
(paperback and hardcover)
The Others, a middle grade fantasy (e-book)
The Sign, a short story (e-book)

Read a new piece of flash fiction each week for free by visiting Jeff's blog:

https://blog.jeffcolemanwrites.com/

About the Author

Jeff Coleman's passion for storytelling goes all the way back to third grade, when he wrote his first (not very good) short story about a leprechaun who enjoys eating green food. While growing up, he was captivated by classic Nintendo games like *Zelda*, and later computer games like *Myst*, each of which took place in worlds very unlike our own, and set his imagination aflame with possibilities for his own tales.

During his college years, Jeff fell in love with math, physics and philosophy, subjects that seeded his heart with a profound interest in the many extraordinary mysteries to be found in apparently ordinary things. Jeff is a firm believer that there is more to the universe than immediate appearances suggest, that there is more to our existence than meets the eye. He's therefore fascinated by stories which probe beyond surface observations, stories which attempt to explore the strange and preternatural, stories which unsettle us, which make us think, which make us question what we are and why we're here.

Some of his favorite books are *The Dark Tower*, by Stephen King; *Neverwhere* and *The Ocean at the End of the Lane*, by Neil Gaiman; *The Night Circus*, by Erin Morgenstern; *The Golem and the Jinni*, by Helene Wecker; *Daughter of Smoke & Bone*, by Laini Taylor; and *Harry Potter*, by J.K. Rowling.